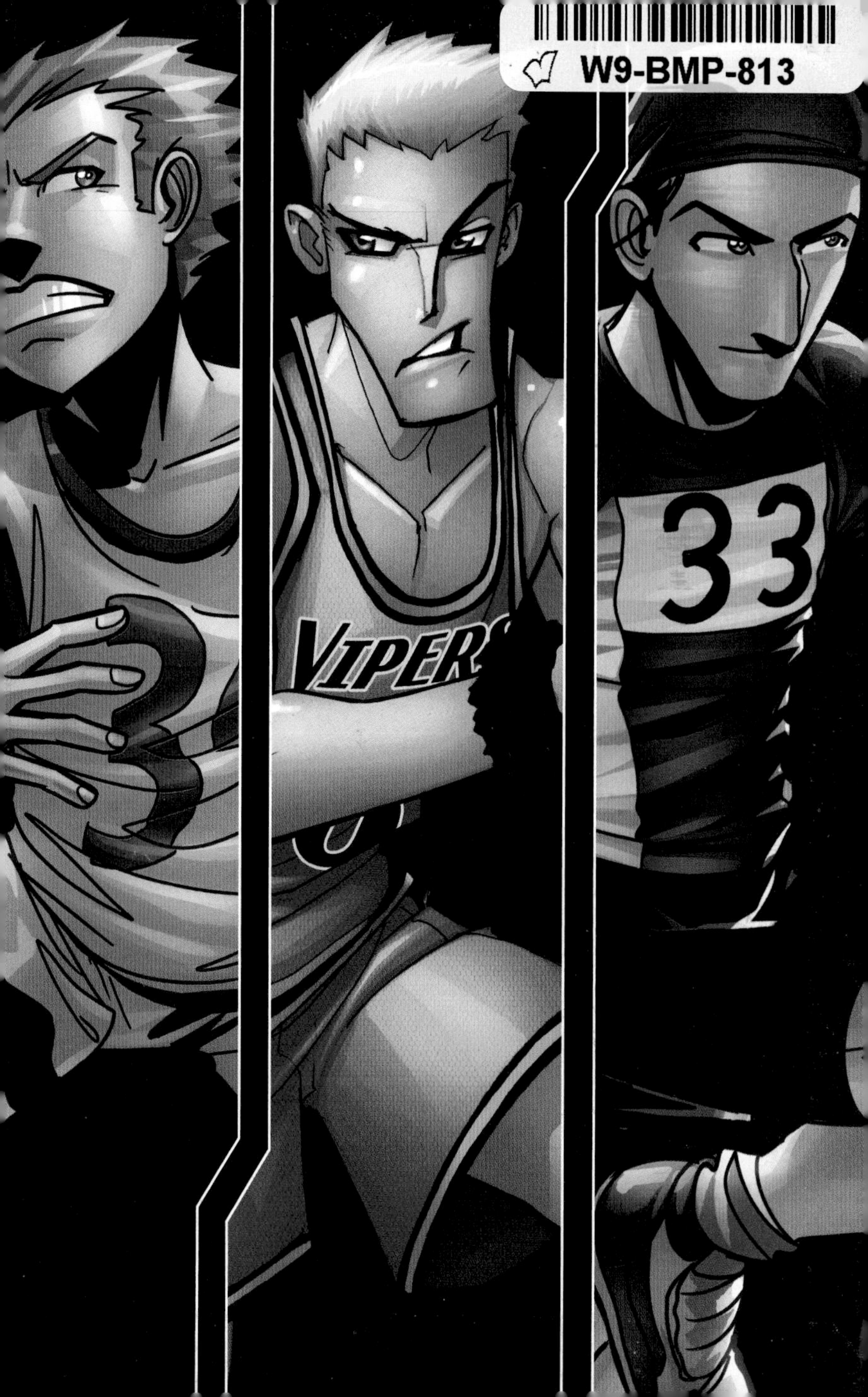
33

UP NEXT ›››

Sports Illustrated KIDS

33

Cheatham Elementary School

TITANS ANNOUNCE TRACK AND FIELD TEAM SIGNUPS BEGINN

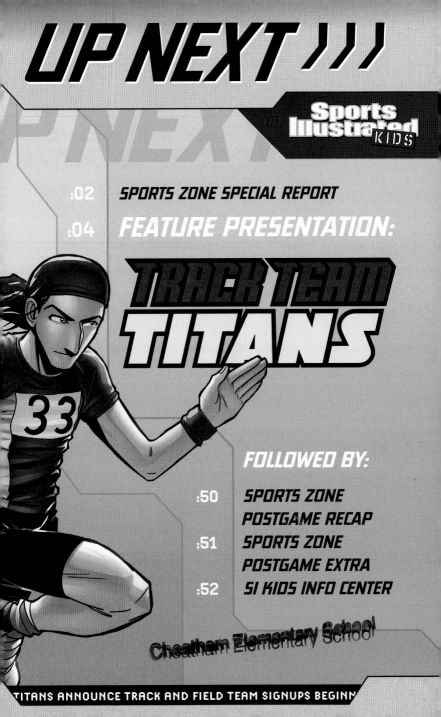

PORTS ZONE

ECIAL REPORT

K

ELD

SCHOOL'S TOP ATHLETES TO TRY OUT FOR TITANS' TRACK TEAM!

76
33

JAKE "SULLY" SULLIVAN

STATS:
AGE: 14
TEAM: TITANS

BIO: The Titans are forming a track team for the first time, and Sully has taken it upon himself to convince the school's most talented teens to join up. There's just one problem — Sully didn't actually ask his friends Chris, Dwight, and Brett for permission before he volunteered them! Now, Sully must convince his hesitant friends to remain on the team, AND turn them into talented track stars...

Sports Illustrated KIDS

UP NEXT: TRACK TEAM TITANS

JAX AND FLYNN ROGERS

AGES: 15
TEAM: GOLIATHS

BIO: Jax and Flynn refer to themselves as "evil twins" mostly because they like to play pranks on everyone. When the Rogers twins are around, no one is safe from their gags.

CHRIS LANDRY

AGE: 14   TEAM: TITANS
BIO: Chris is the school's best football player. He's known as a touchdown-tossing quarterback who thrives under pressure.

CHRIS

DWIGHT REYNOLDS

AGE: 14   TEAM: TITANS
BIO: Dwight can outjump anybody on the court. At 14, he can already leap and reach the basketball rim.

DWIGHT

BRETT PULASKI

AGE: 14   TEAM: TITANS
BIO: Brett is the school's best baseball player. He's known as a speedy baserunner who never backs down.

BRETT

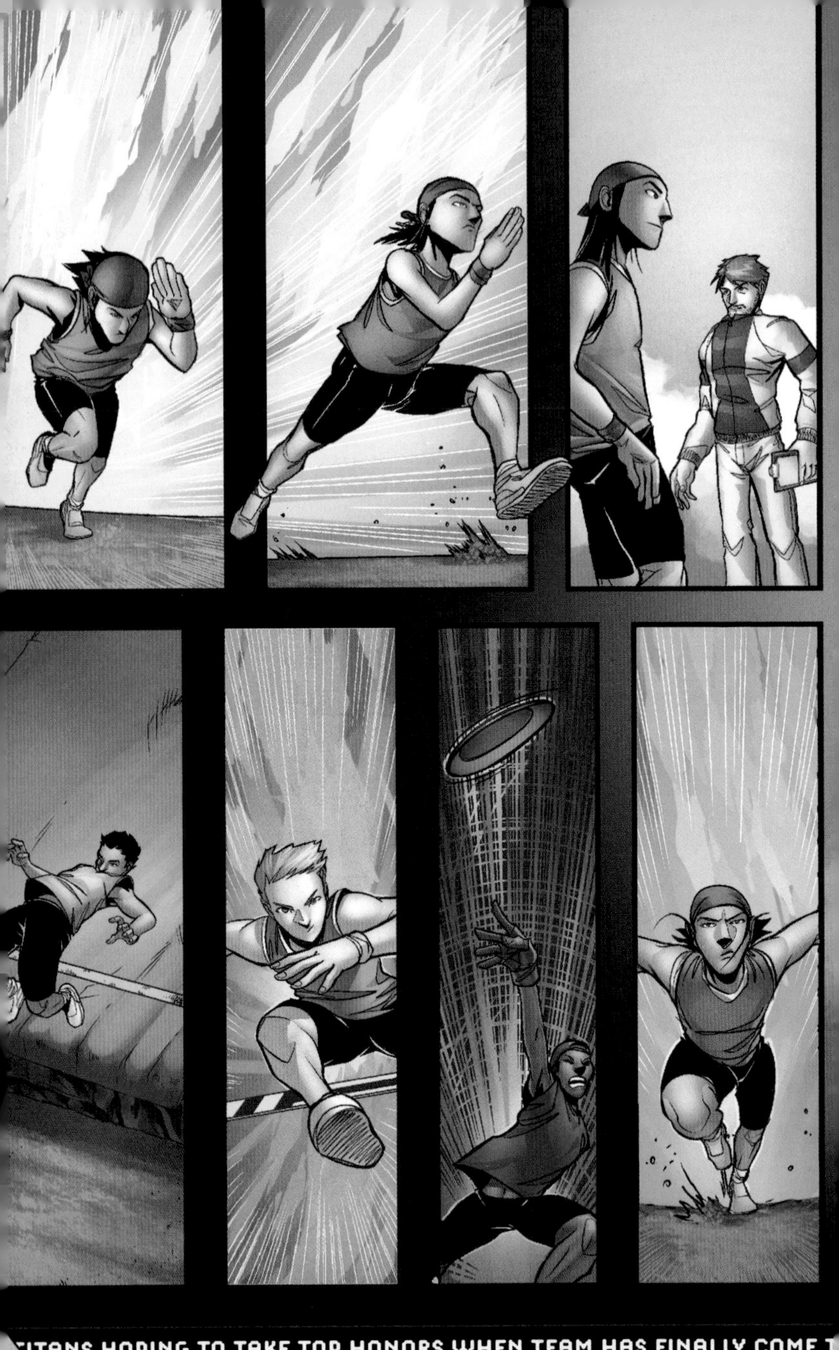
HOPING TO TAKE TOP HONORS WHEN TEAM HAS FINALLY COME

Sports Illustrated KIDS

PRESENTS

TRACK TEAM TITANS

A PRODUCTION OF

STONE ARCH BOOKS
a capstone imprint

written by Stephanie True Peters
illustrated by Jesus Aburto
inked by Andres Esparza
colored by Fernando Cano

designed and directed by Bob Lentz
edited by Sean Tulien
creative direction by Heather Kindseth
editorial management by Donald Lemke
editorial direction by Michael Dahl

ports Illustrated KIDS *Track Team Titans* is published by Stone Arch Books,
51 Good Counsel Drive, P.O. Box 669, Mankato, Minnesota 56002.
www.capstonepub.com

rinted in the United States of America in Stevens Point, Wisconsin.
92010 005934WZS11

Summary: Track season is about to begin, and Sully is ready and raring to run. But on the first day of tryouts, no other students show up! If the Titans don't get more members, there won't be a track team. So Sully pays a visit to the other sports teams, hoping their star athletes will join. None of the other athletes think much of track and field. Sully will have to beat them at their own sports to change their minds . . .

Library of Congress Cataloging-in-Publication Data
Peters, Stephanie True, 1965-
Track team titans / written by Stephanie True Peters ; illustrated by Aburtov, Andres Esparza, and Fares Maese.
p. cm. -- (Sports Illustrated kids graphic novels)
ISBN 978-1-4342-2224-4 (library binding) -- ISBN 978-1-4342-3072-0 (pbk.)
1. Graphic novels. [1. Graphic novels. 2. Track and field--Fiction. 3. Athletes--Fiction.] I. Aburto, Jesus, ill. II. Esparza, Andres, ill. III. Maese, Fares, ill. IV. Title.
PZ7.7.P44Tr 2011
741.5'973--dc22
2010032922

NUPS ARE STILL SEVERAL NAMES SHORT OF A FULL TRACK TE SIK TICKER

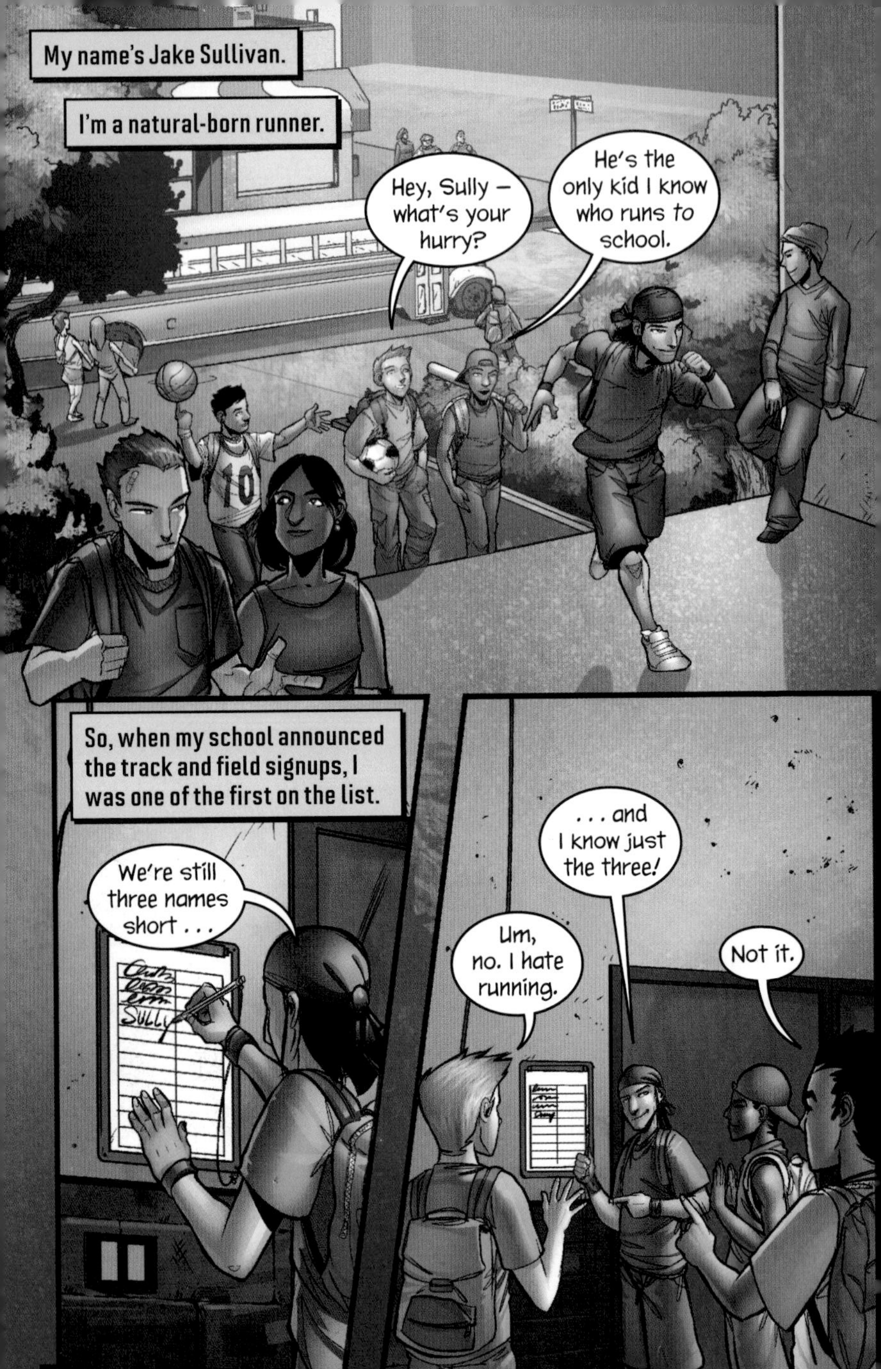
My name's Jake Sullivan.
I'm a natural-born runner.
Hey, Sully — what's your hurry?
He's the only kid I know who runs to school.
So, when my school announced the track and field signups, I was one of the first on the list.
We're still three names short . . .
. . . and I know just the three!
Um, no. I hate running.
Not it.

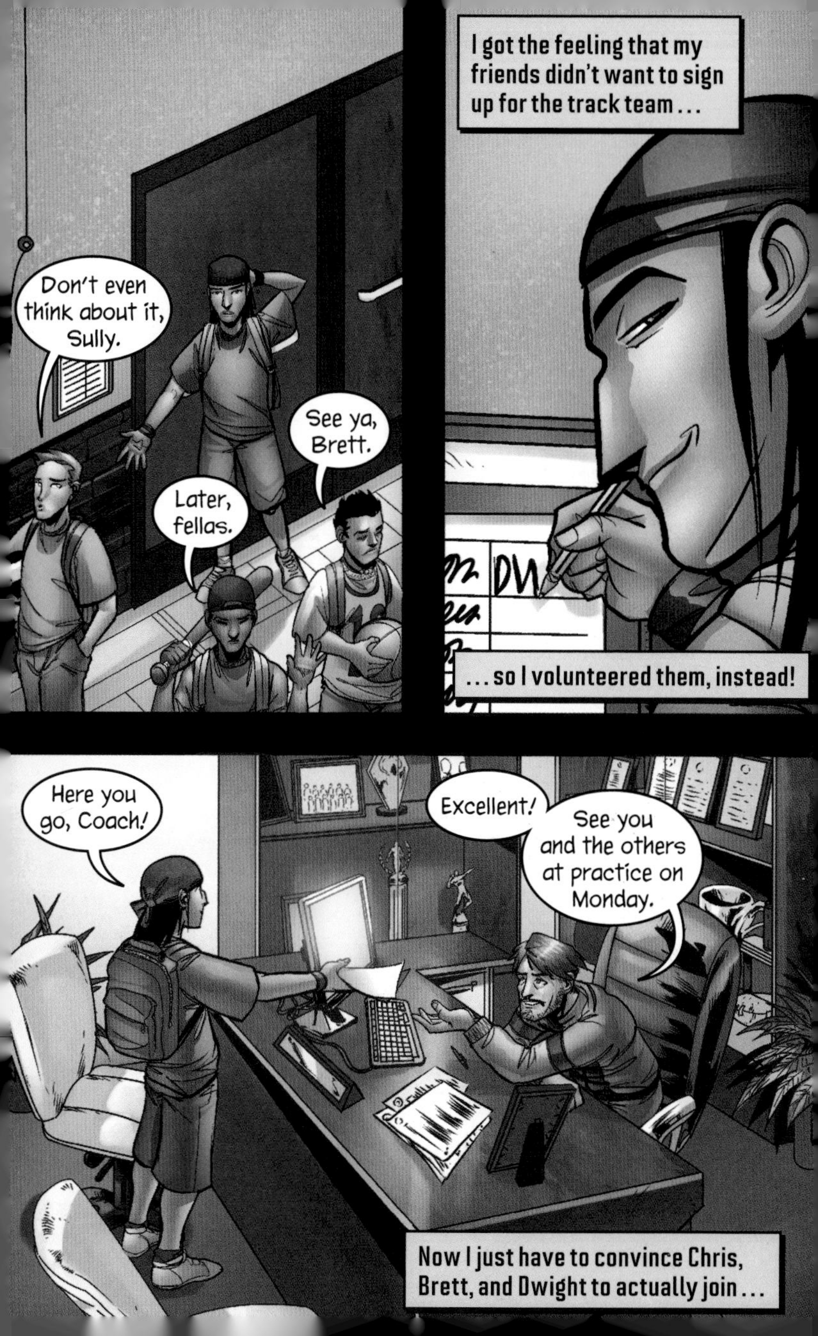
Don't even think about it, Sully.
Later, fellas.
See ya, Brett.
I got the feeling that my friends didn't want to sign up for the track team . . .
. . . so I volunteered them, instead!
Here you go, Coach!
Excellent!
See you and the others at practice on Monday.
Now I just have to convince Chris, Brett, and Dwight to actually join . . .

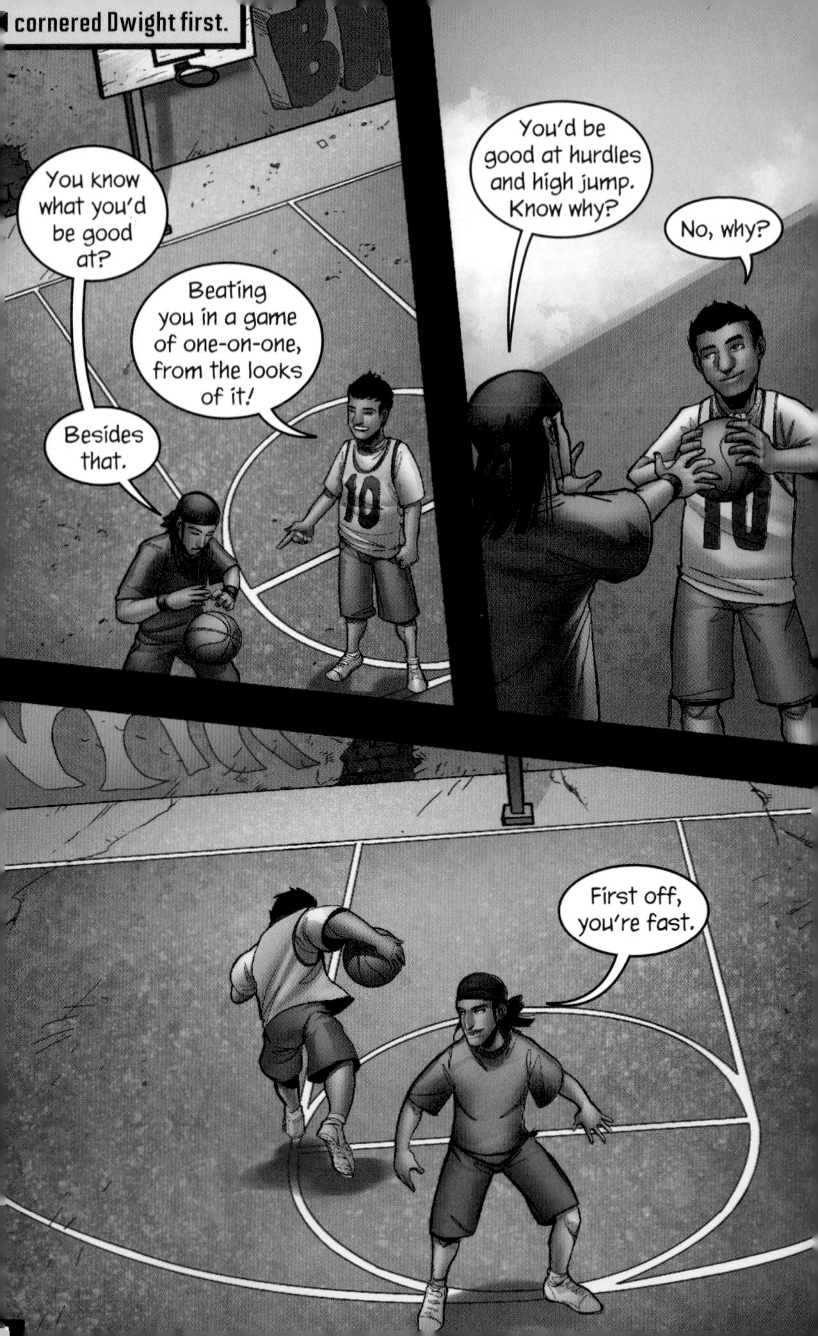
cornered Dwight first.
You know what you'd be good at?
Beating you in a game of one-on-one, from the looks of it!
Besides that.
You'd be good at hurdles and high jump. Know why?
No, why?
First off, you're fast.

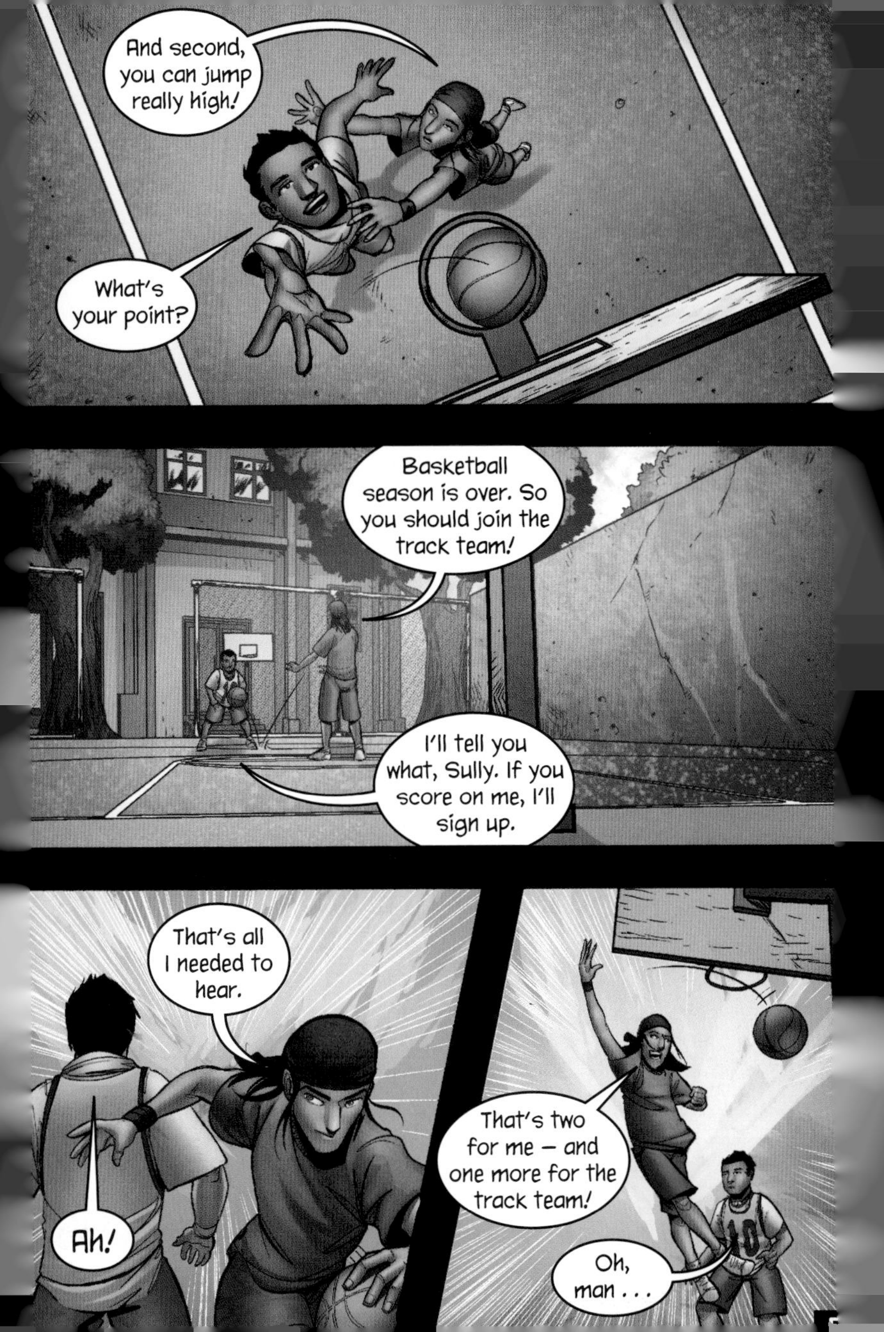
And second, you can jump really high!
What's your point?
Basketball season is over. So you should join the track team!
I'll tell you what, Sully. If you score on me, I'll sign up.
That's all I needed to hear.
Ah!
That's two for me — and one more for the track team!
Oh, man . . .

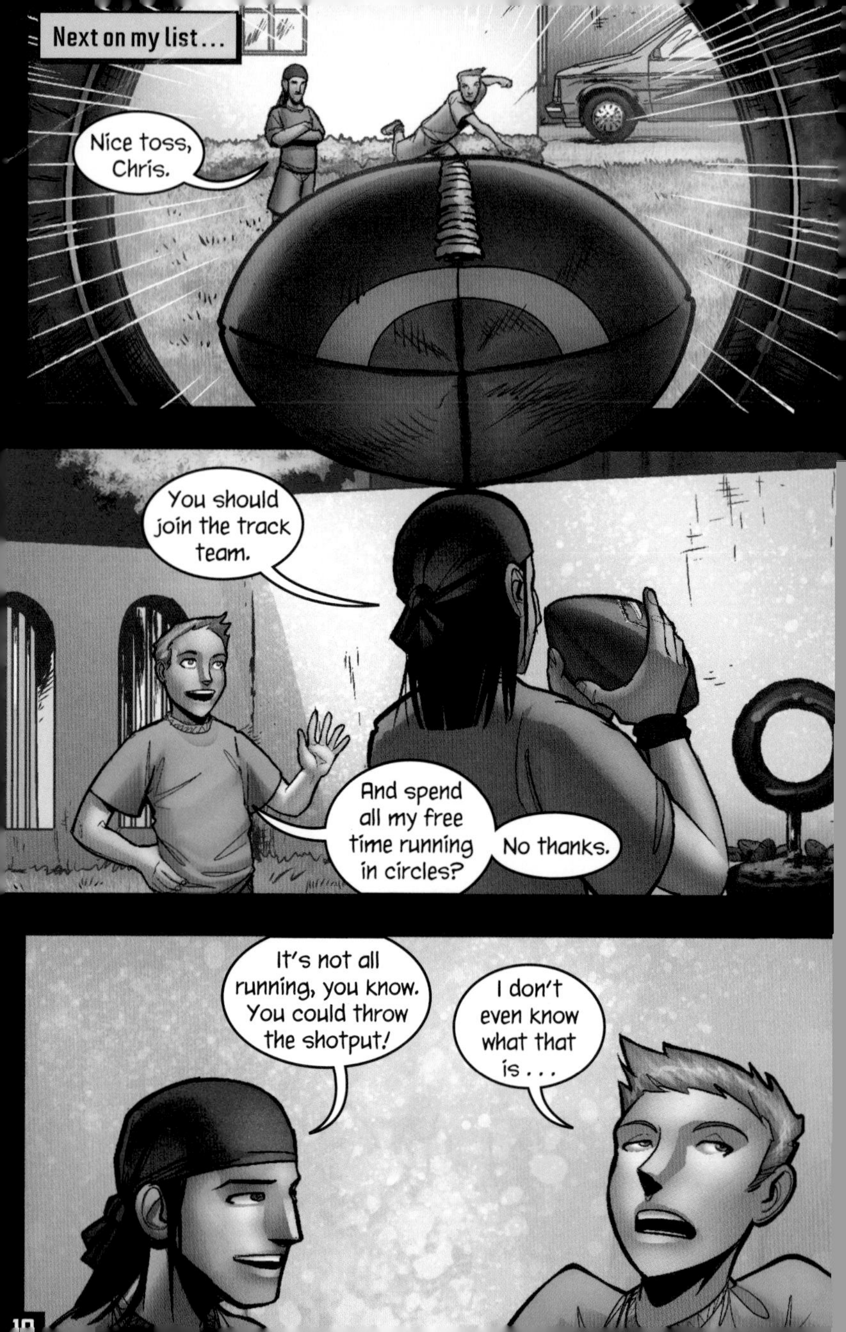
Next on my list . . .
Nice toss, Chris.
You should join the track team.
And spend all my free time running in circles?
No thanks.
It's not all running, you know. You could throw the shotput!
I don't even know what that is . . .

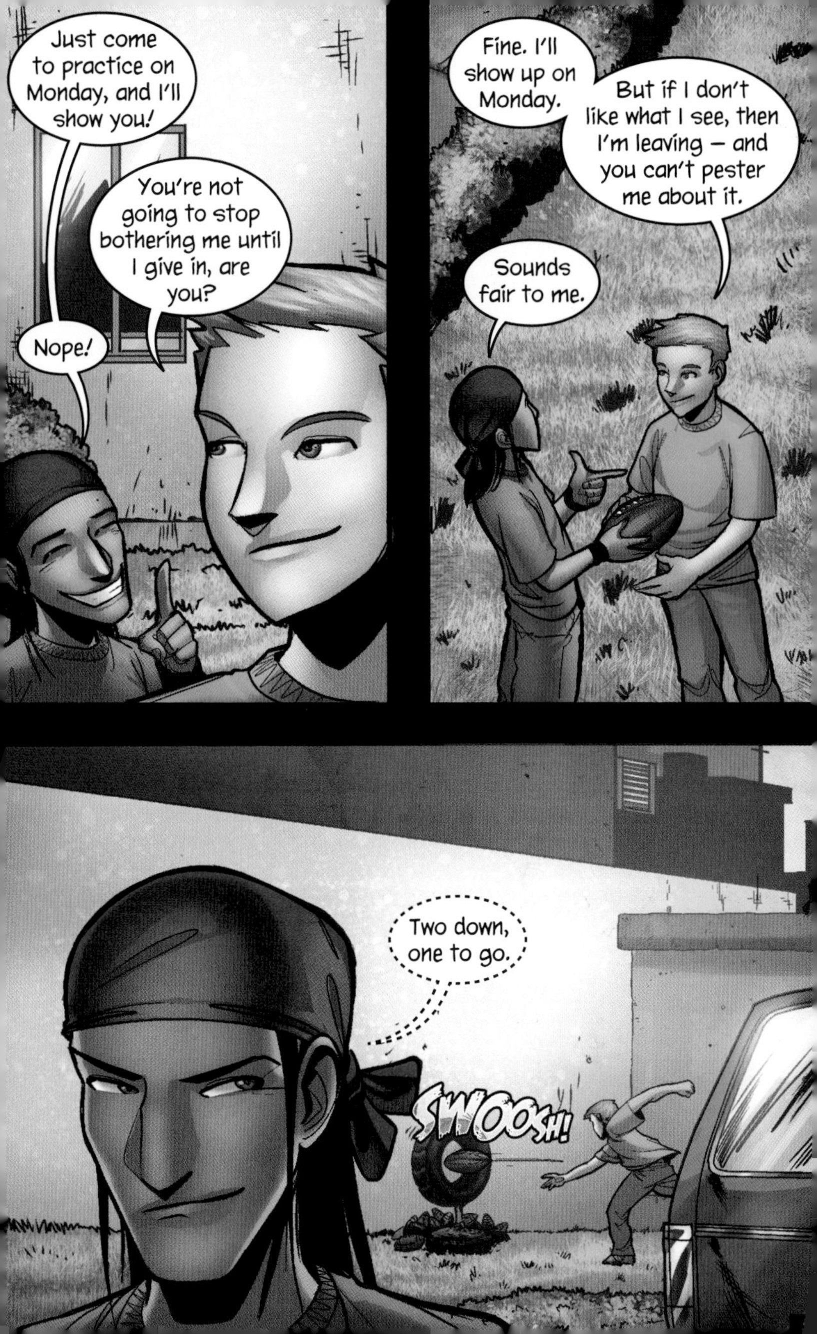
Just come to practice on Monday, and I'll show you!
You're not going to stop bothering me until I give in, are you?
Nope!
Fine. I'll show up on Monday.
But if I don't like what I see, then I'm leaving — and you can't pester me about it.
Sounds fair to me.
Two down, one to go.
SWOOSH!

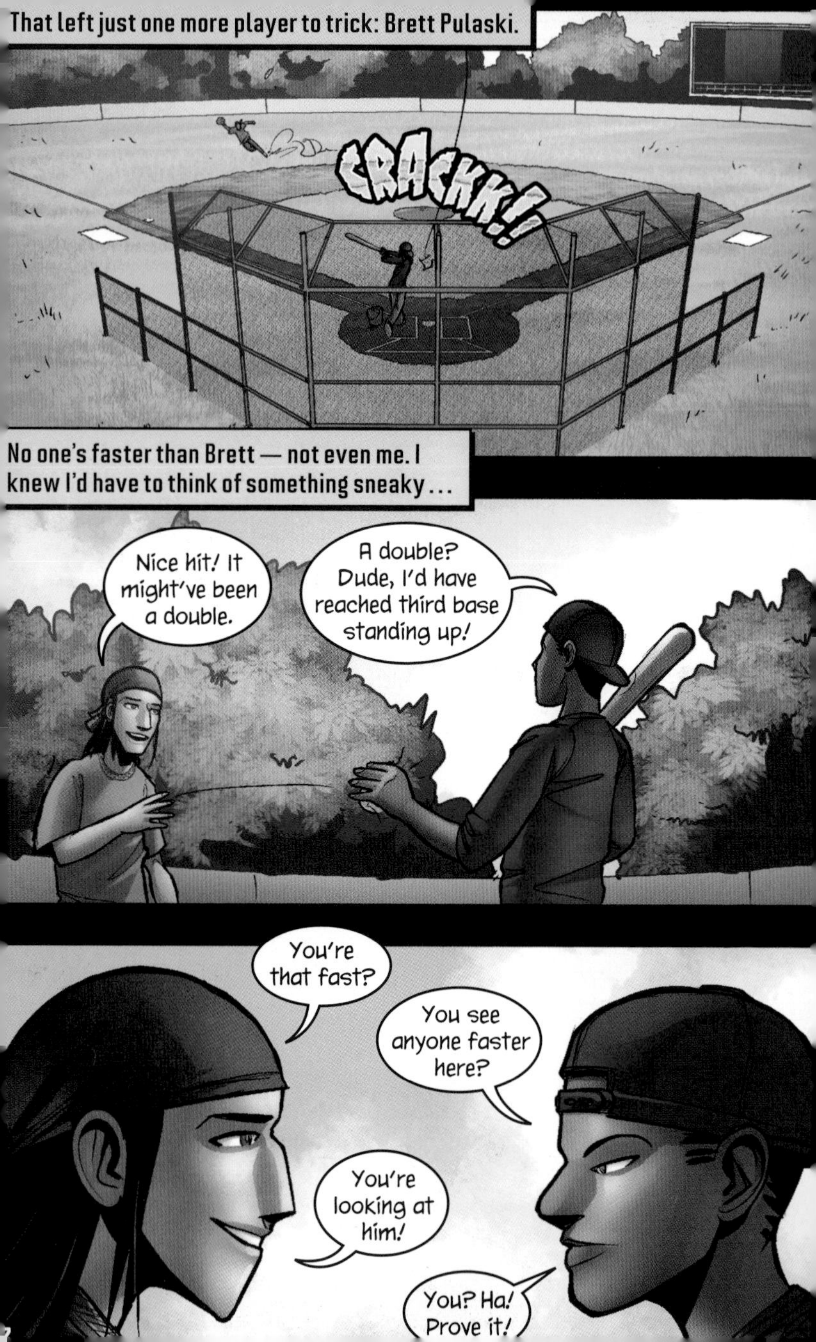

That left just one more player to trick: Brett Pulaski.
CRACKK!!
No one's faster than Brett — not even me. I knew I'd have to think of something sneaky . . .
Nice hit! It might've been a double.
A double? Dude, I'd have reached third base standing up!
You're that fast?
You see anyone faster here?
You're looking at him!
You? Ha! Prove it!

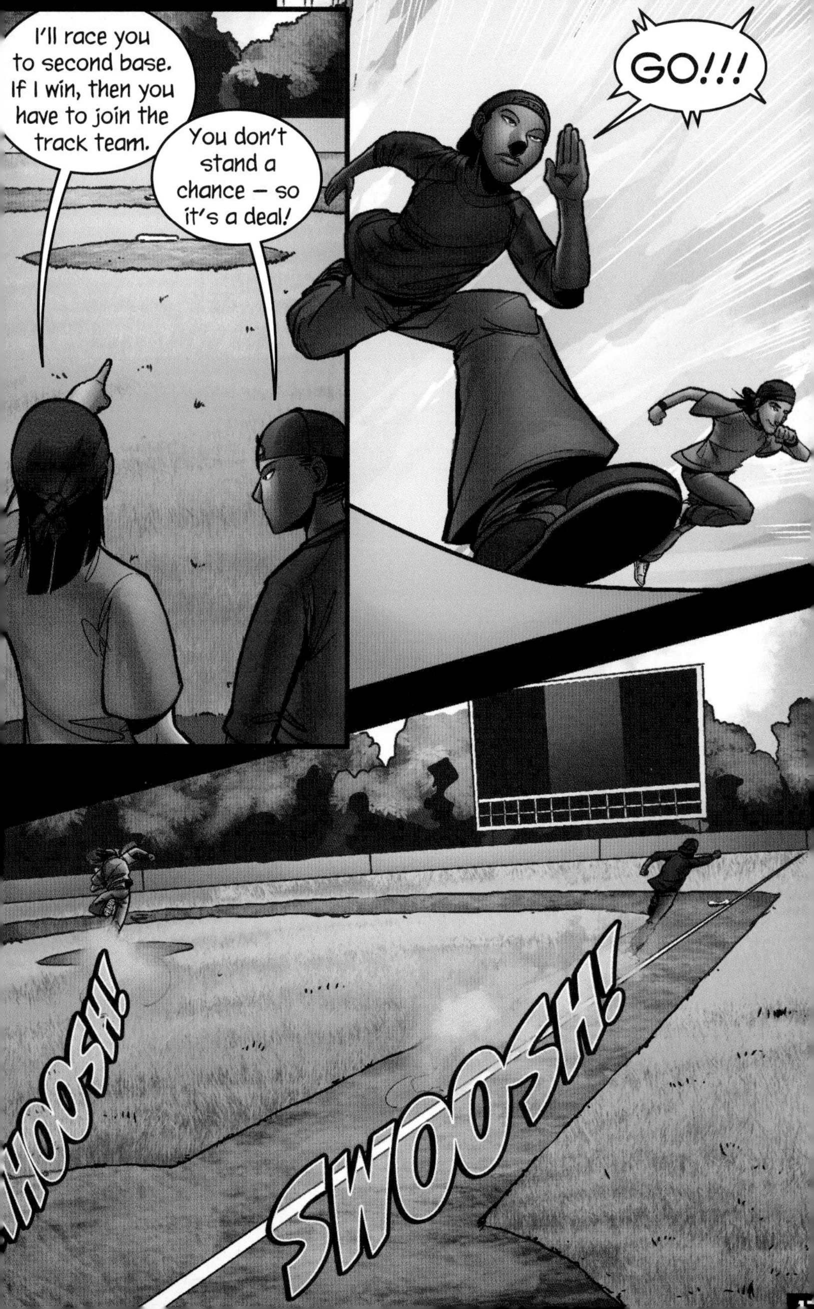
I'll race you to second base. If I win, then you have to join the track team.
You don't stand a chance — so it's a deal!
GO!!!
WHOOSH!
SWOOSH!

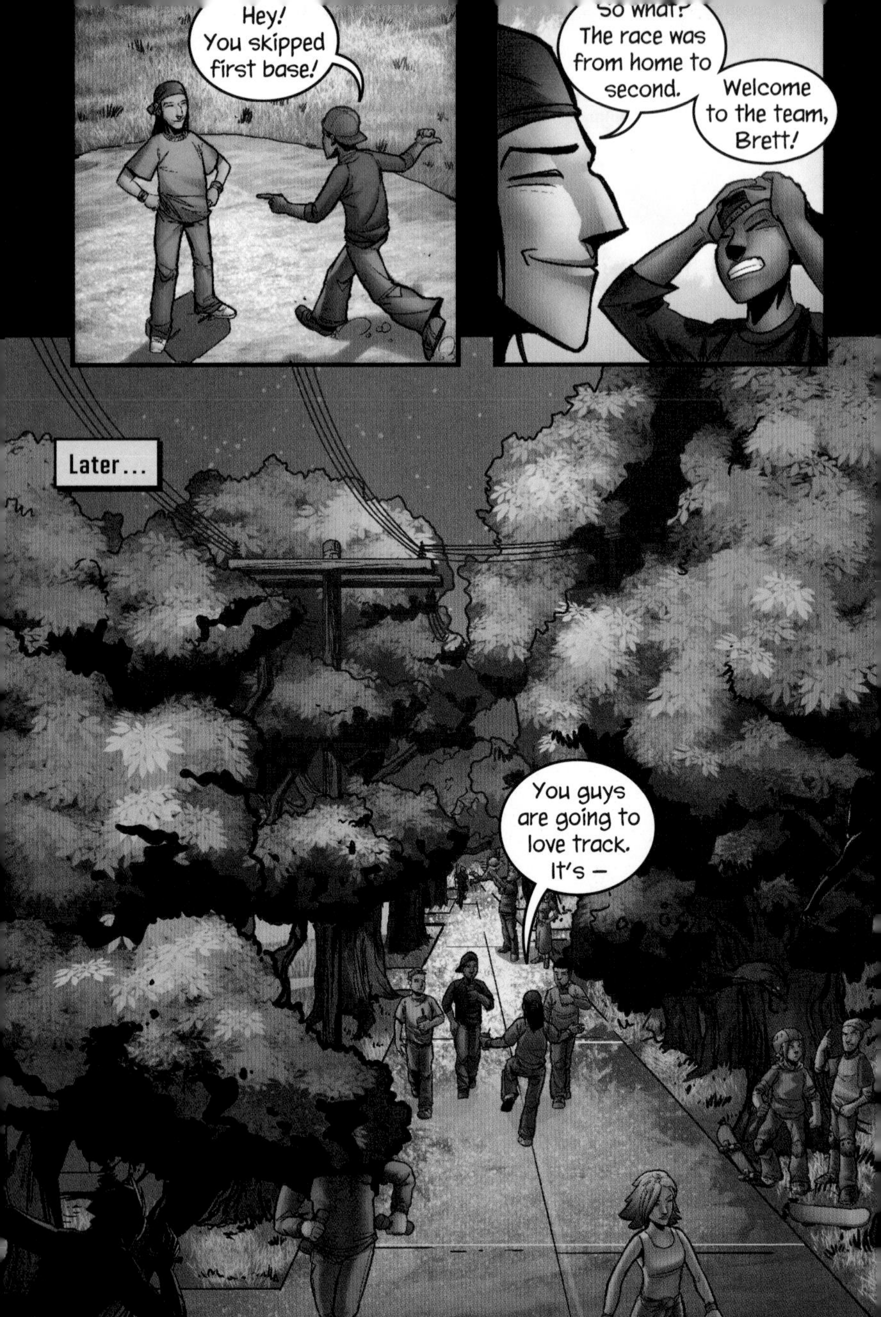
Hey! You skipped first base!
So what? The race was from home to second.
Welcome to the team, Brett!
Later...
You guys are going to love track. It's —

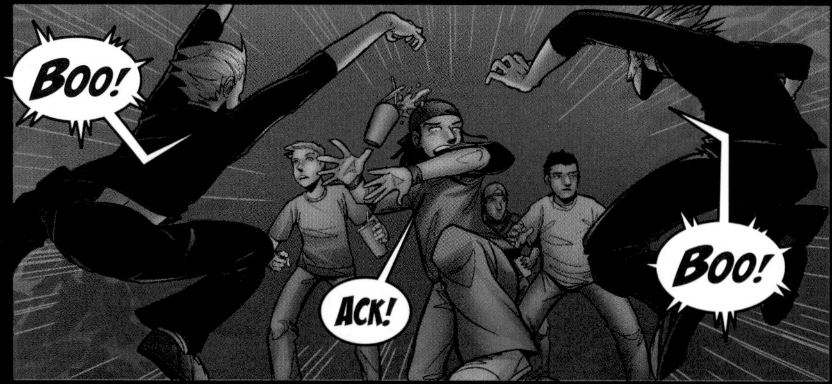
BOO!
ACK!
BOO!

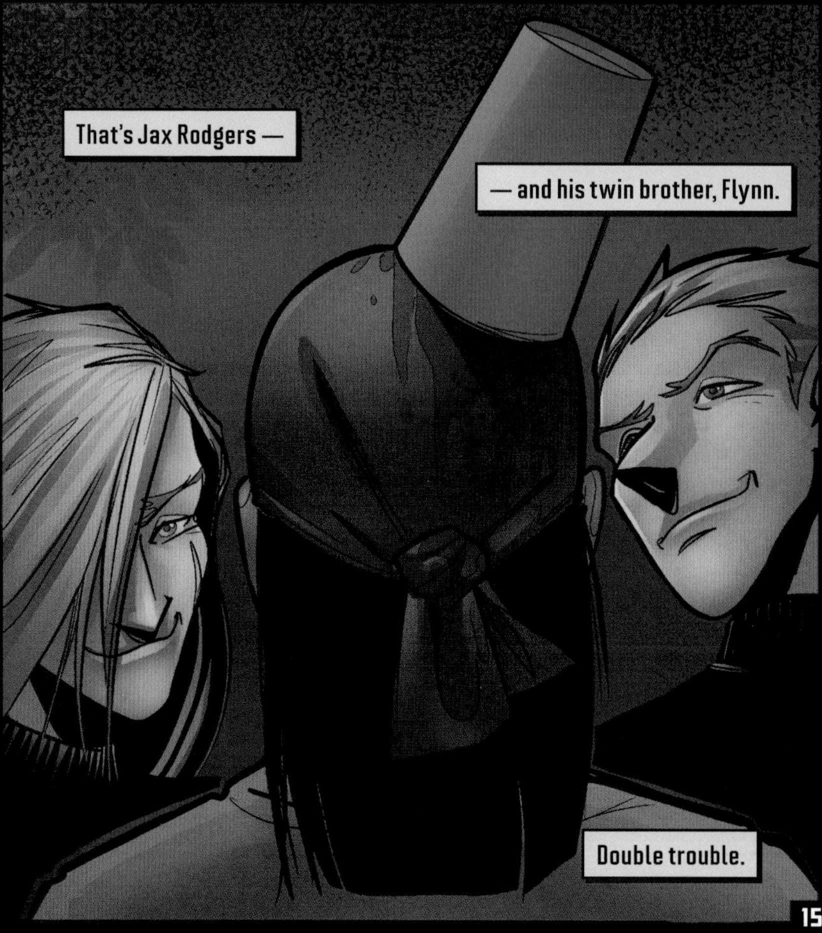
That's Jax Rodgers —
— and his twin brother, Flynn.
Double trouble.

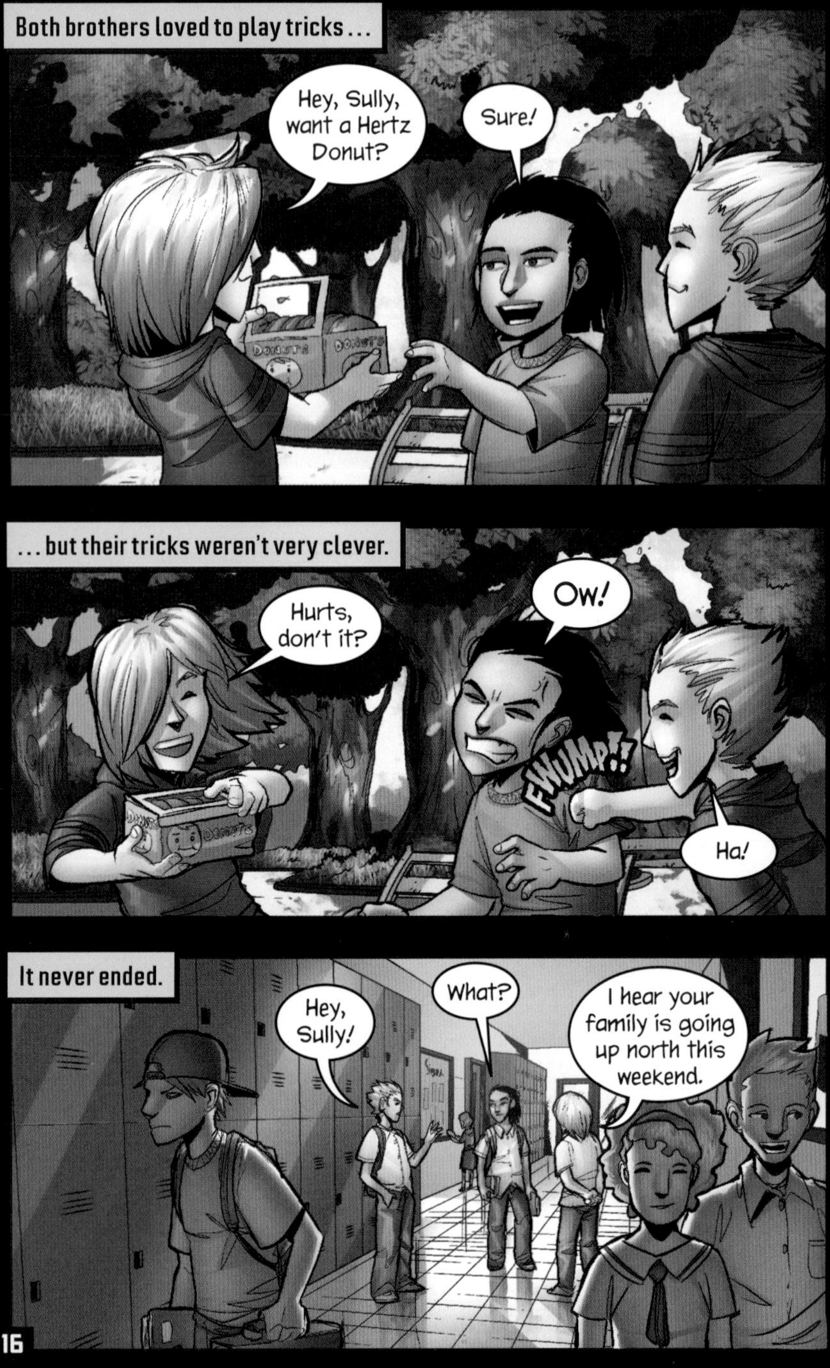
Both brothers loved to play tricks . . .
Hey, Sully, want a Hertz Donut?
Sure!
. . . but their tricks weren't very clever.
Hurts, don't it?
Ow!
FWUMP!!
Ha!
It never ended.
Hey, Sully!
What?
I hear your family is going up north this weekend.

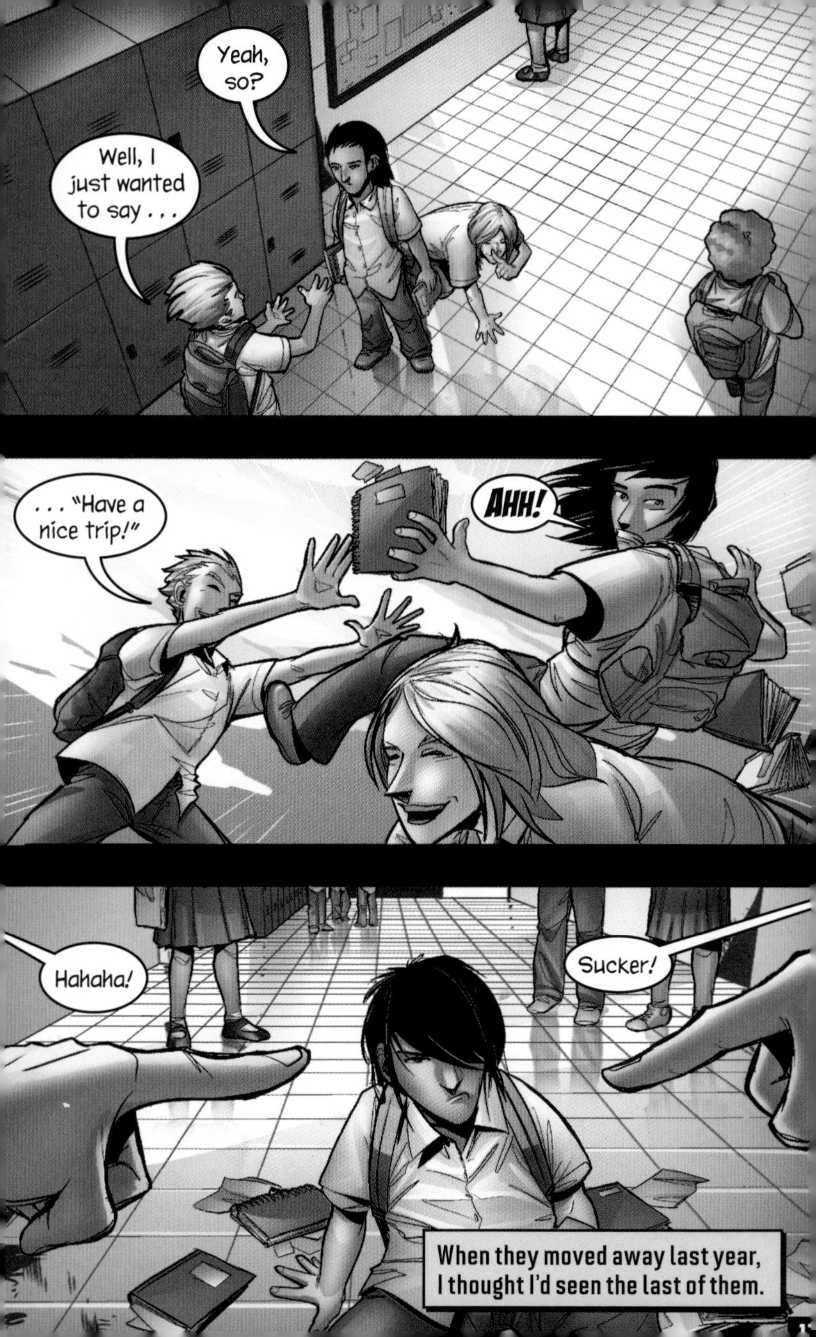
Yeah, so?
Well, I just wanted to say . . .
. . . "Have a nice trip!"
AHH!
Hahaha!
Sucker!
When they moved away last year, I thought I'd seen the last of them.

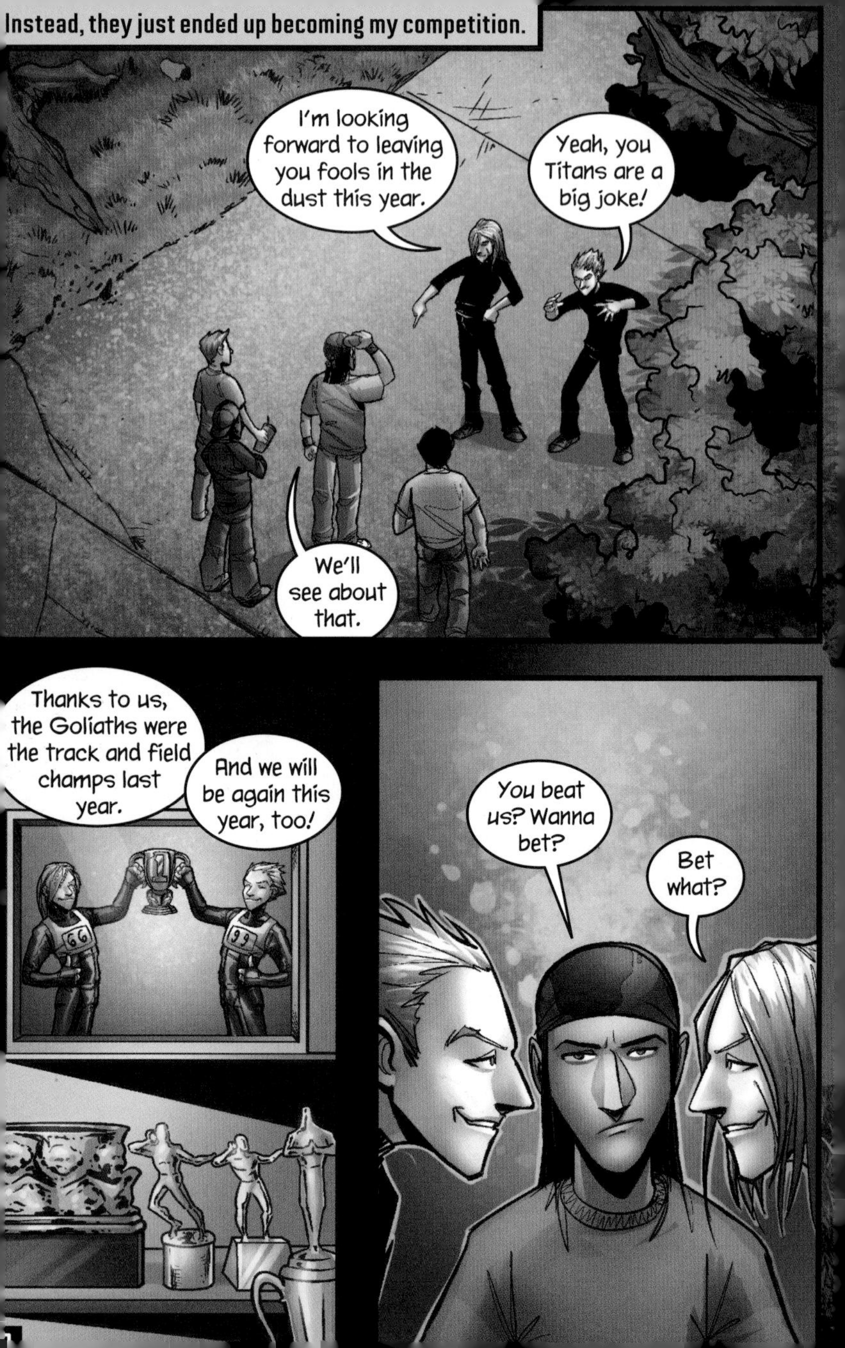
Instead, they just ended up becoming my competition.
I'm looking forward to leaving you fools in the dust this year.
Yeah, you Titans are a big joke!
We'll see about that.
Thanks to us, the Goliaths were the track and field champs last year.
And we will be again this year, too!
66
99
You beat us? Wanna bet?
Bet what?

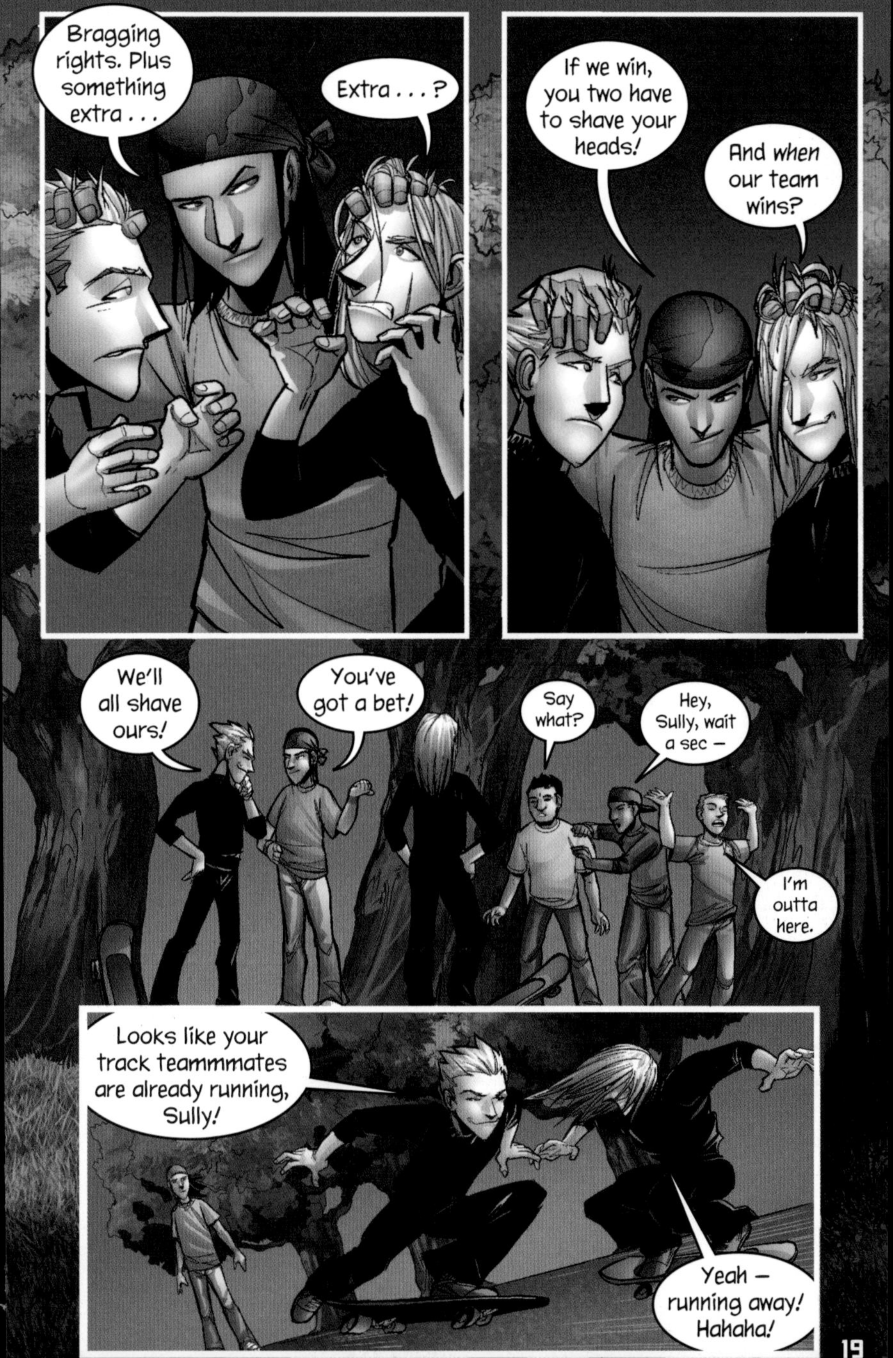
Bragging rights. Plus something extra . . .
Extra . . . ?
If we win, you two have to shave your heads!
And when our team wins?
We'll all shave ours!
You've got a bet!
Say what?
Hey, Sully, wait a sec —
I'm outta here.
Looks like your track teammmates are already running, Sully!
Yeah — running away! Hahaha!

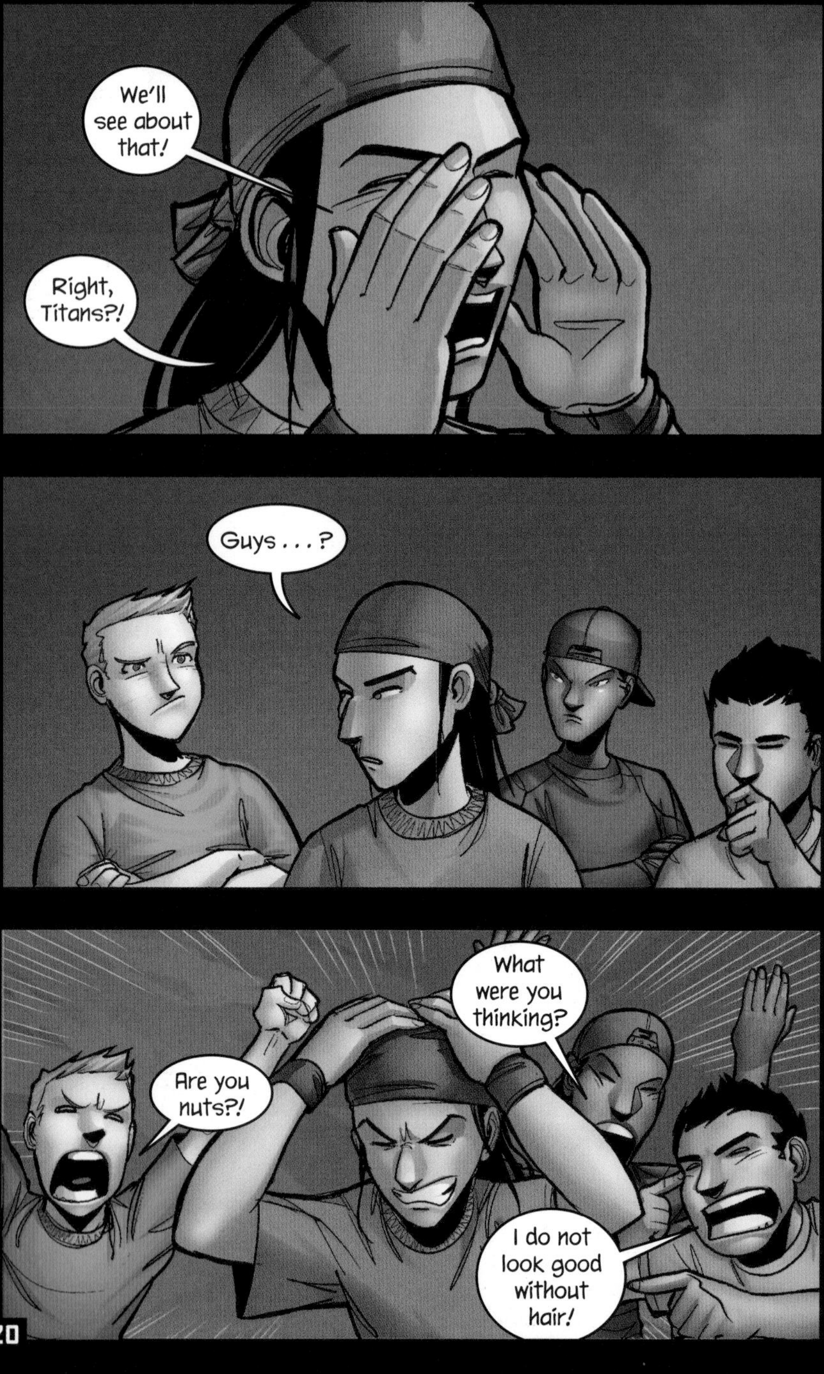
We'll see about that!
Right, Titans?!
Guys . . . ?
What were you thinking?
Are you nuts?!
I do not look good without hair!

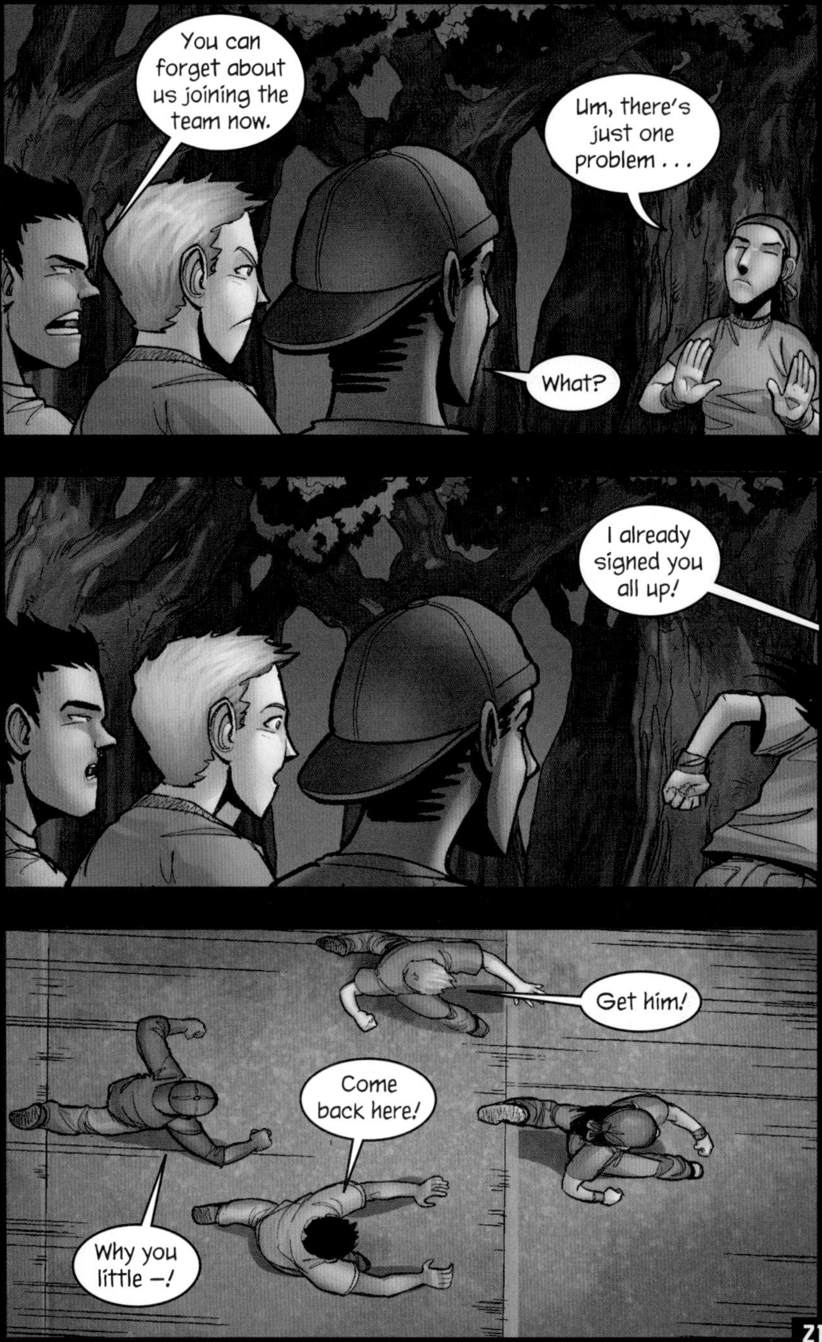
You can forget about us joining the team now.
Um, there's just one problem . . .
What?
I already signed you all up!
Get him!
Come back here!
Why you little —!

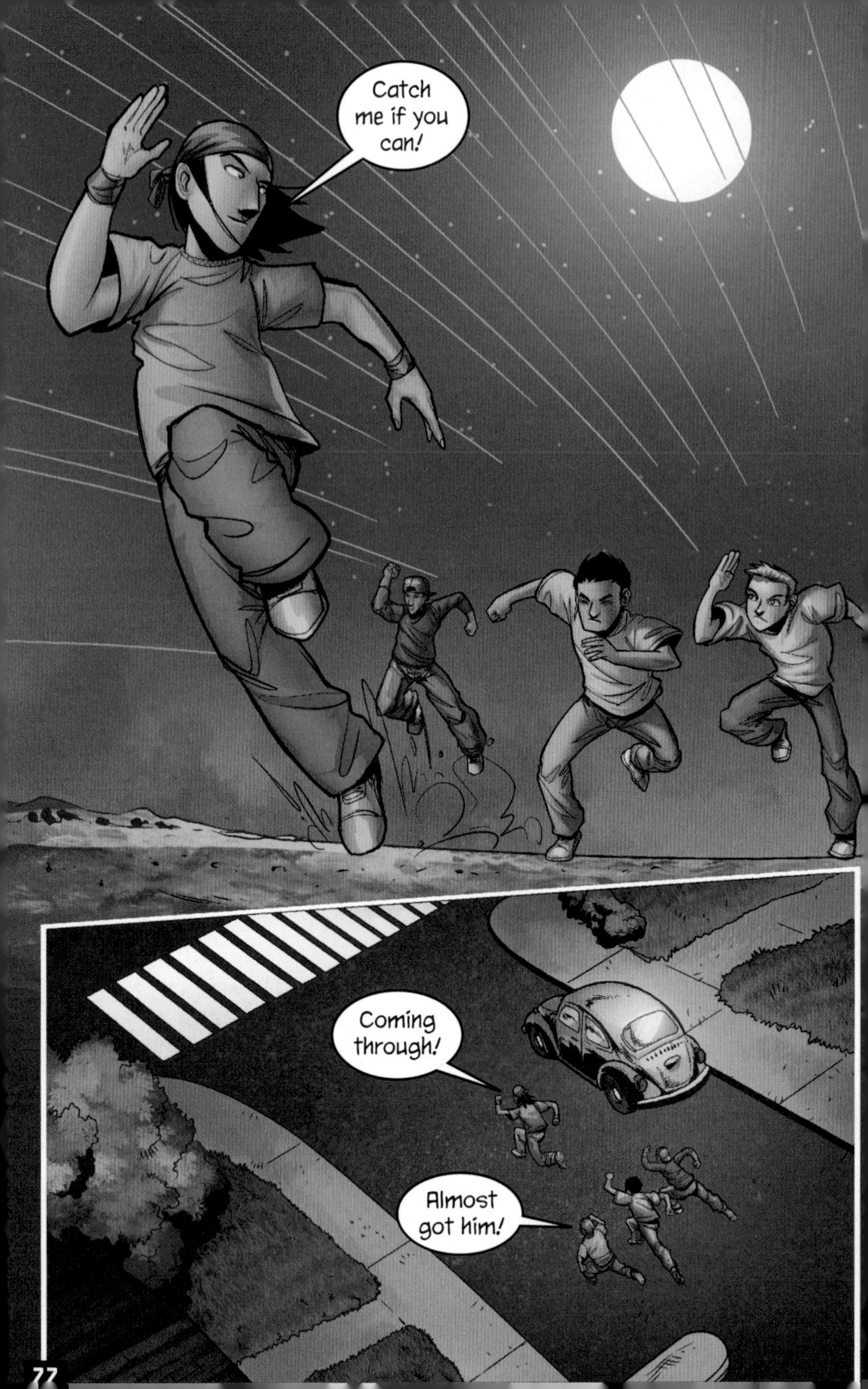
Catch me if you can!
Coming through!
Almost got him!

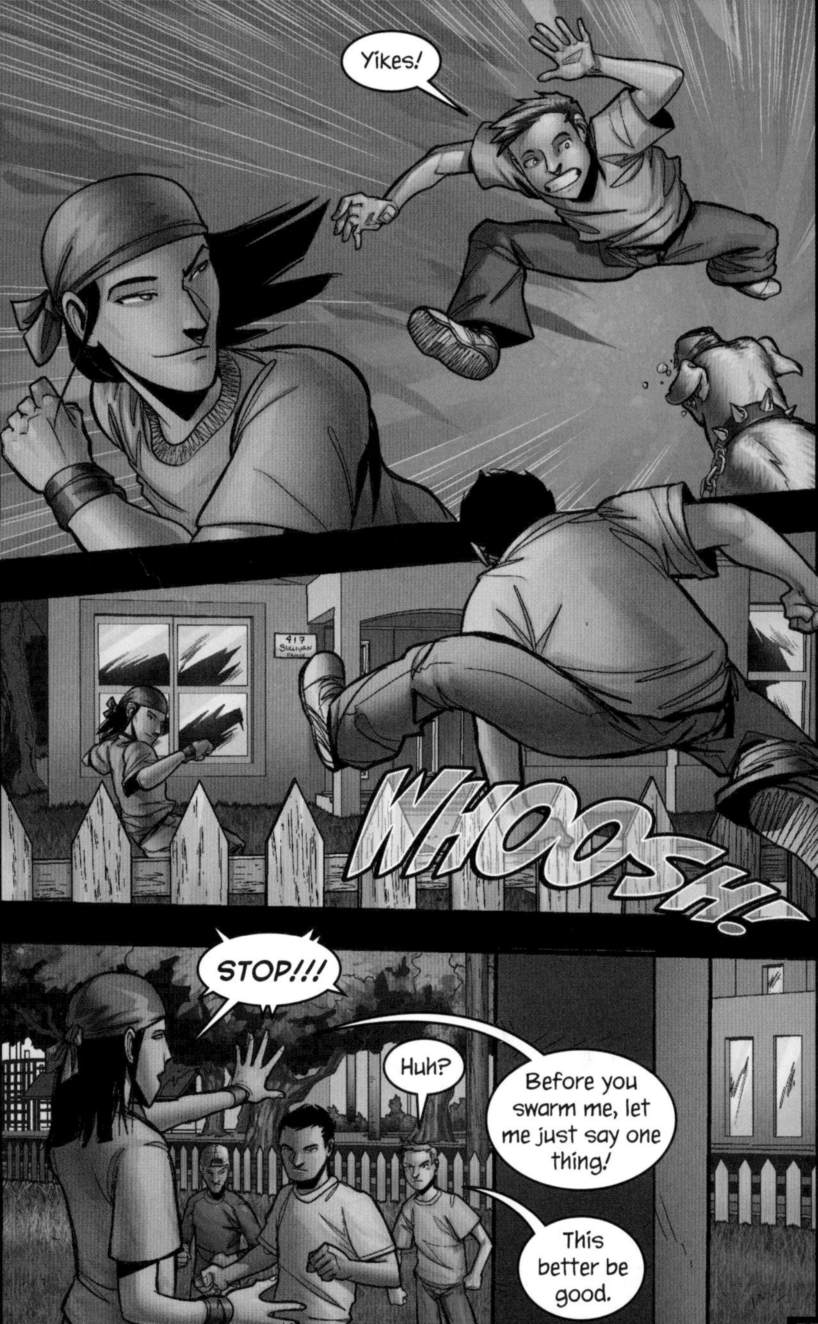
Yikes!
WHOOSH!
STOP!!!
Huh?
Before you swarm me, let me just say one thing!
This better be good.

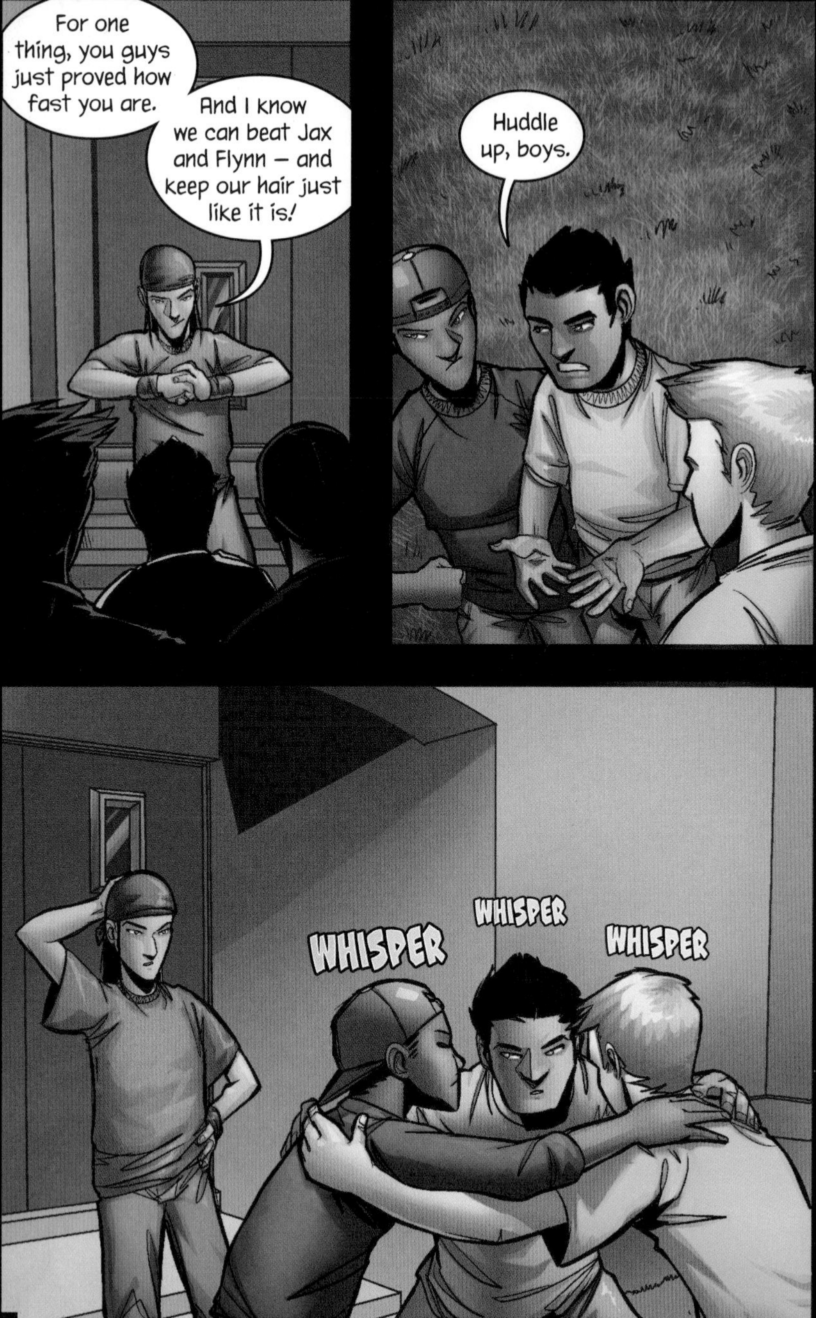
For one thing, you guys just proved how fast you are.
And I know we can beat Jax and Flynn — and keep our hair just like it is!
Huddle up, boys.
WHISPER
WHISPER
WHISPER

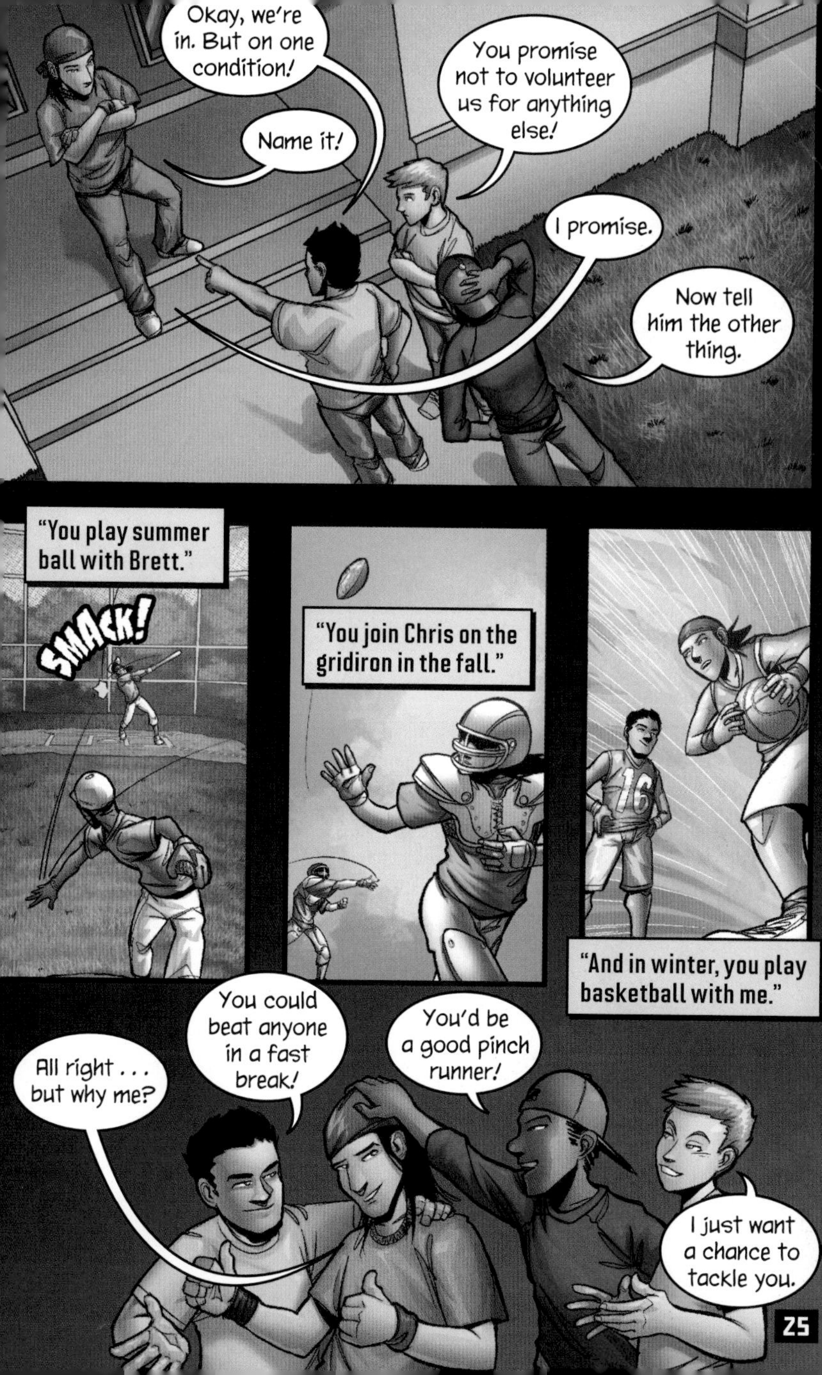

Okay, we're in. But on one condition!
Name it!
You promise not to volunteer us for anything else!
I promise.
Now tell him the other thing.
"You play summer ball with Brett."
SMACK!
"You join Chris on the gridiron in the fall."
"And in winter, you play basketball with me."
All right . . . but why me?
You could beat anyone in a fast break!
You'd be a good pinch runner!
I just want a chance to tackle you.

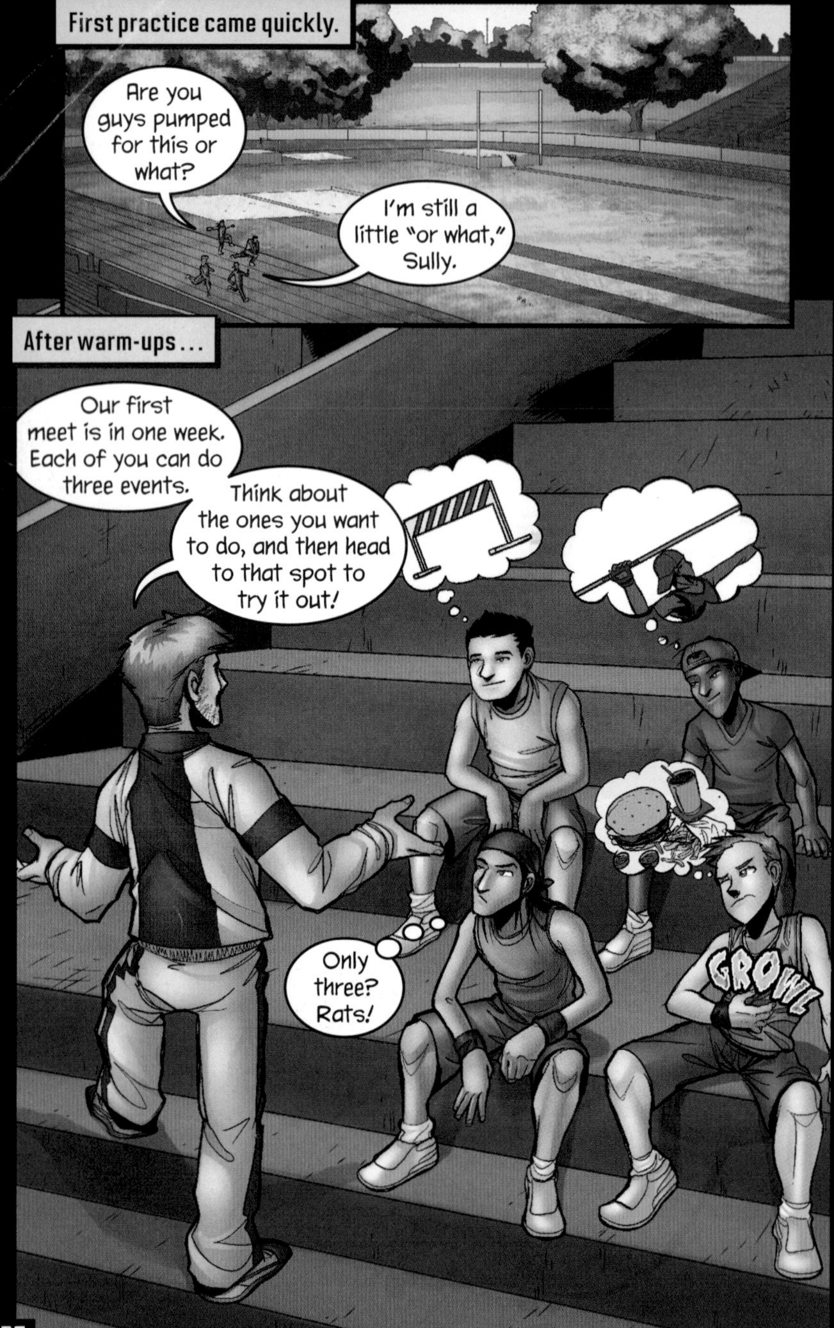
First practice came quickly.
Are you guys pumped for this or what?
I'm still a little "or what," Sully.
After warm-ups . . .
Our first meet is in one week. Each of you can do three events.
Think about the ones you want to do, and then head to that spot to try it out!
Only three? Rats!
GROWL

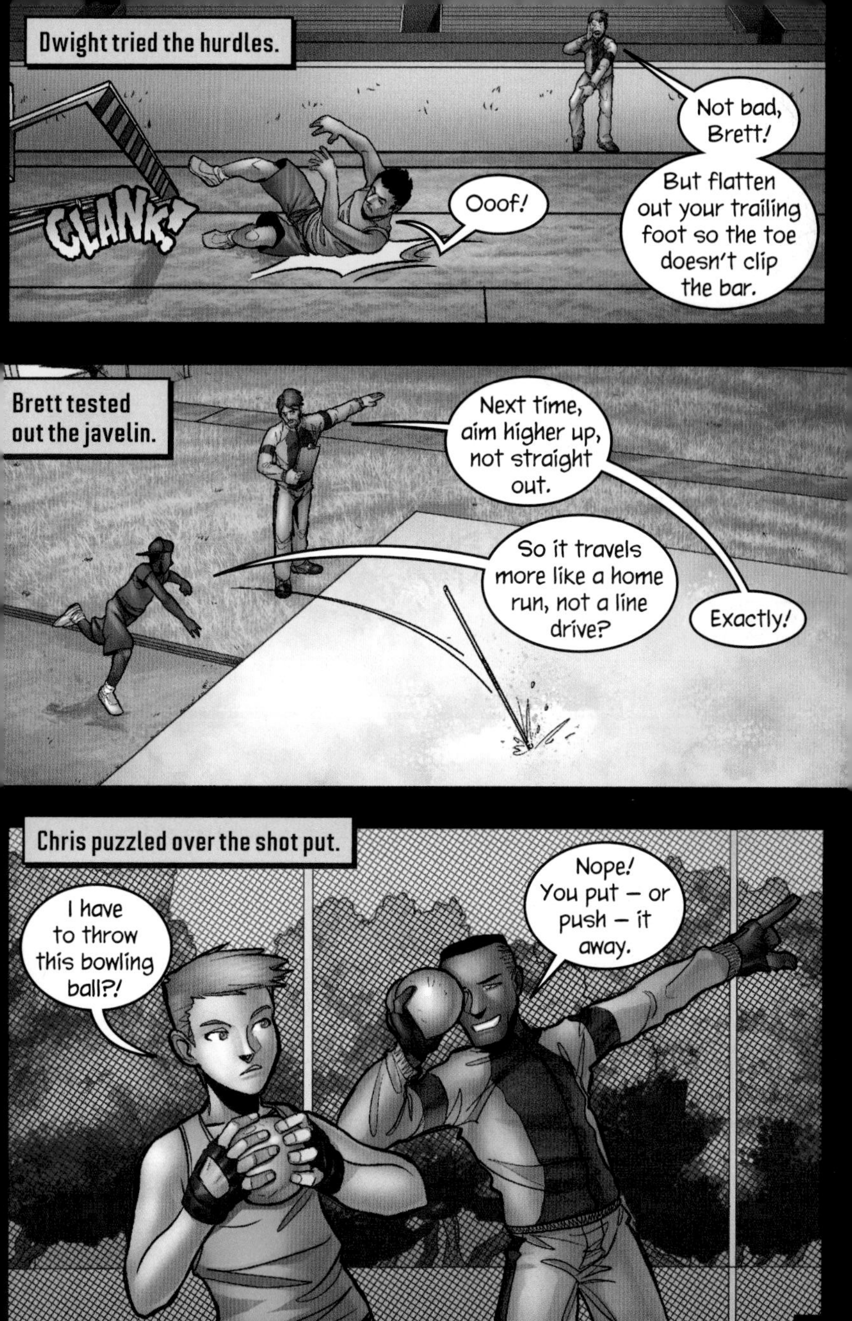
Dwight tried the hurdles.
CLANK!
Ooof!
Not bad, Brett!
But flatten out your trailing foot so the toe doesn't clip the bar.
Brett tested out the javelin.
Next time, aim higher up, not straight out.
So it travels more like a home run, not a line drive?
Exactly!
Chris puzzled over the shot put.
I have to throw this bowling ball?!
Nope! You put — or push — it away.

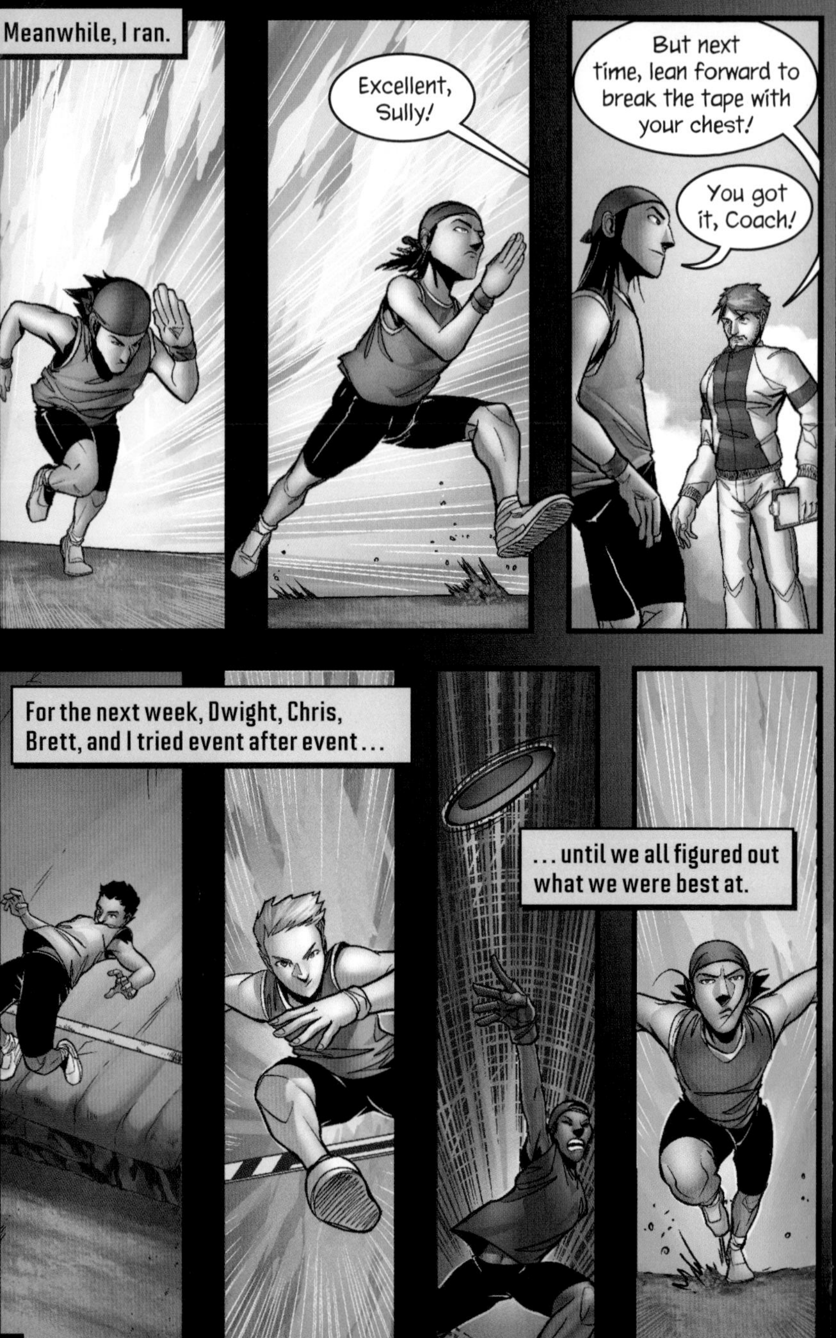
Meanwhile, I ran.
Excellent, Sully!
But next time, lean forward to break the tape with your chest!
You got it, Coach!
For the next week, Dwight, Chris, Brett, and I tried event after event . . .
. . . until we all figured out what we were best at.

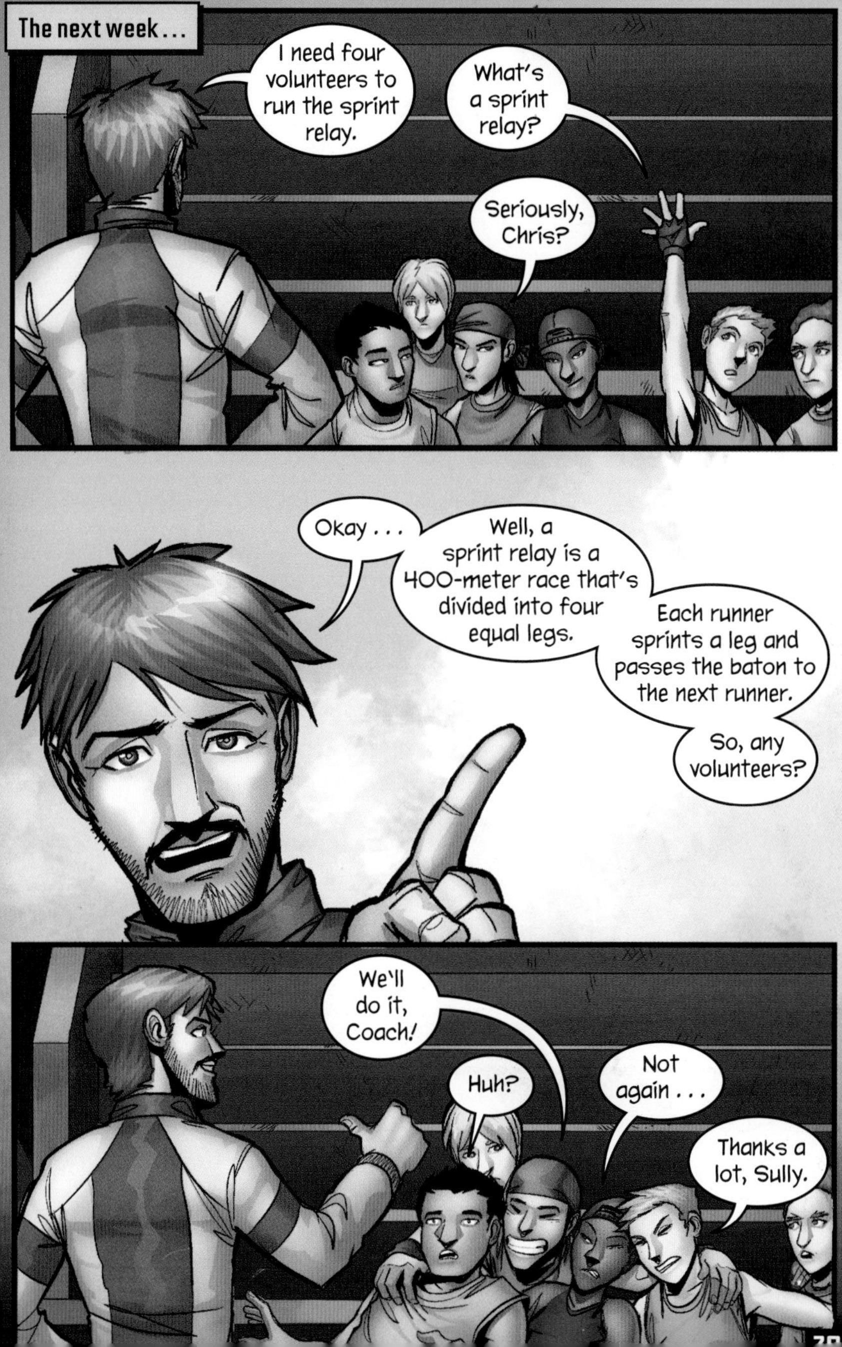
The next week . . .
I need four volunteers to run the sprint relay.
What's a sprint relay?
Seriously, Chris?
Okay . . .
Well, a sprint relay is a 400-meter race that's divided into four equal legs.
Each runner sprints a leg and passes the baton to the next runner.
So, any volunteers?
We'll do it, Coach!
Huh?
Not again . . .
Thanks a lot, Sully.

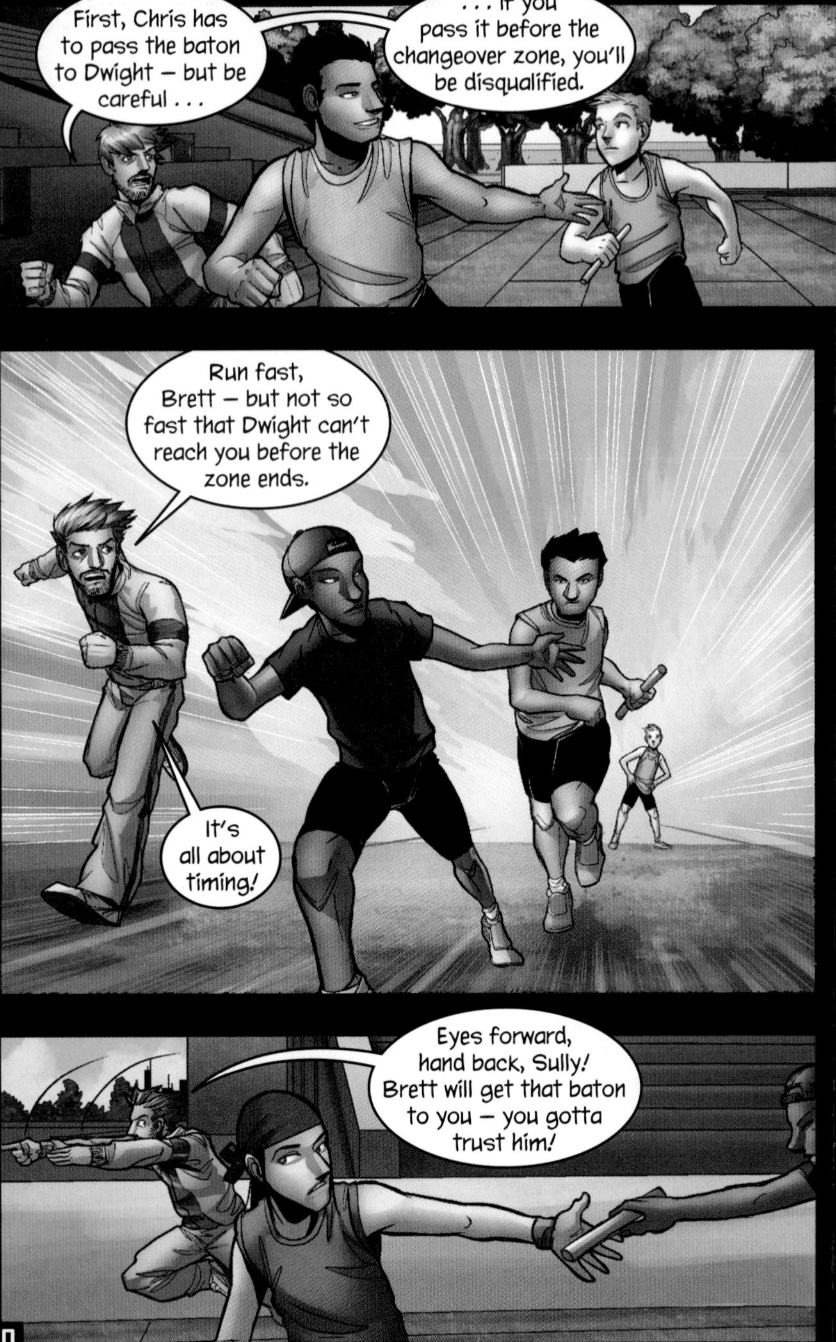
First, Chris has to pass the baton to Dwight — but be careful . . .
. . . if you pass it before the changeover zone, you'll be disqualified.
Run fast, Brett — but not so fast that Dwight can't reach you before the zone ends.
It's all about timing!
Eyes forward, hand back, Sully! Brett will get that baton to you — you gotta trust him!

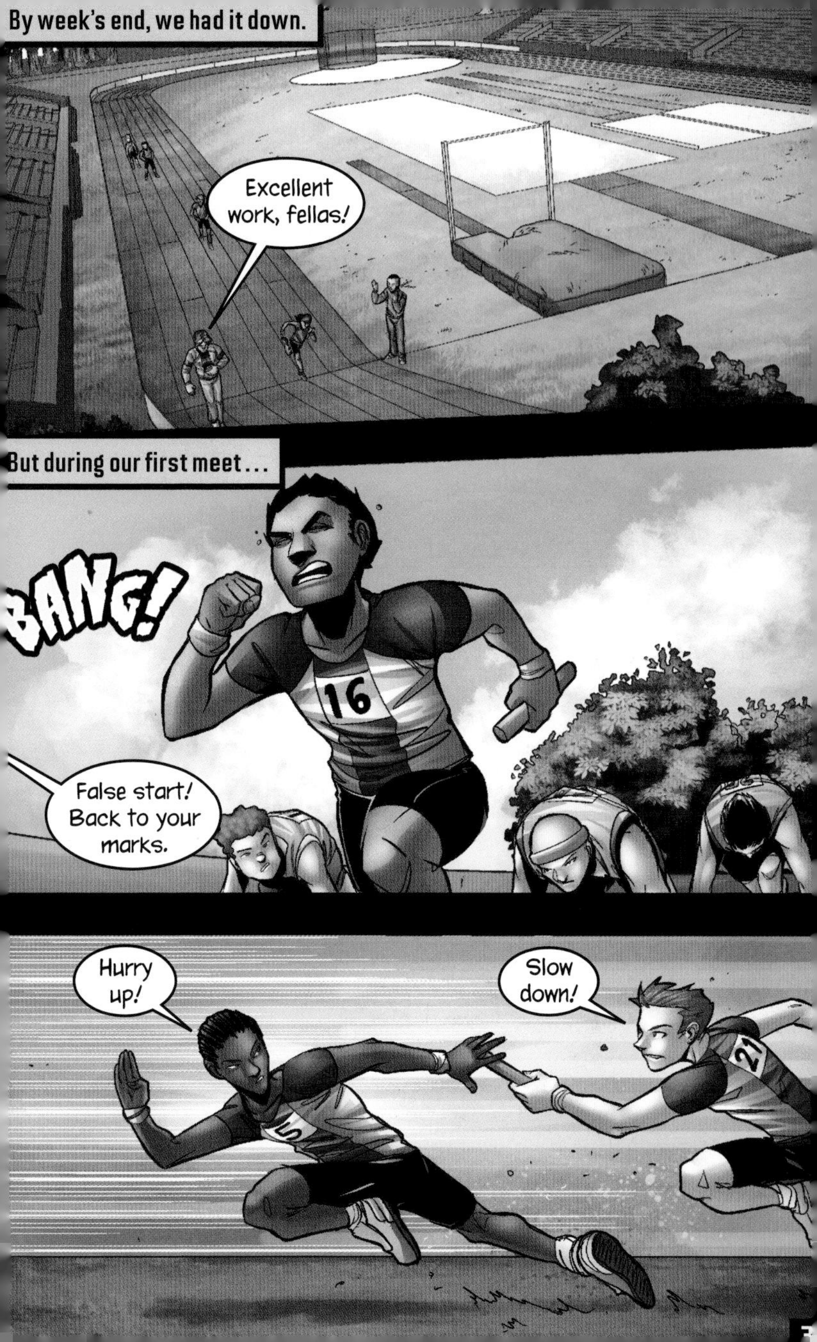
By week's end, we had it down.
Excellent work, fellas!
But during our first meet . . .
BANG!
16
False start! Back to your marks.
Hurry up!
Slow down!
5
21

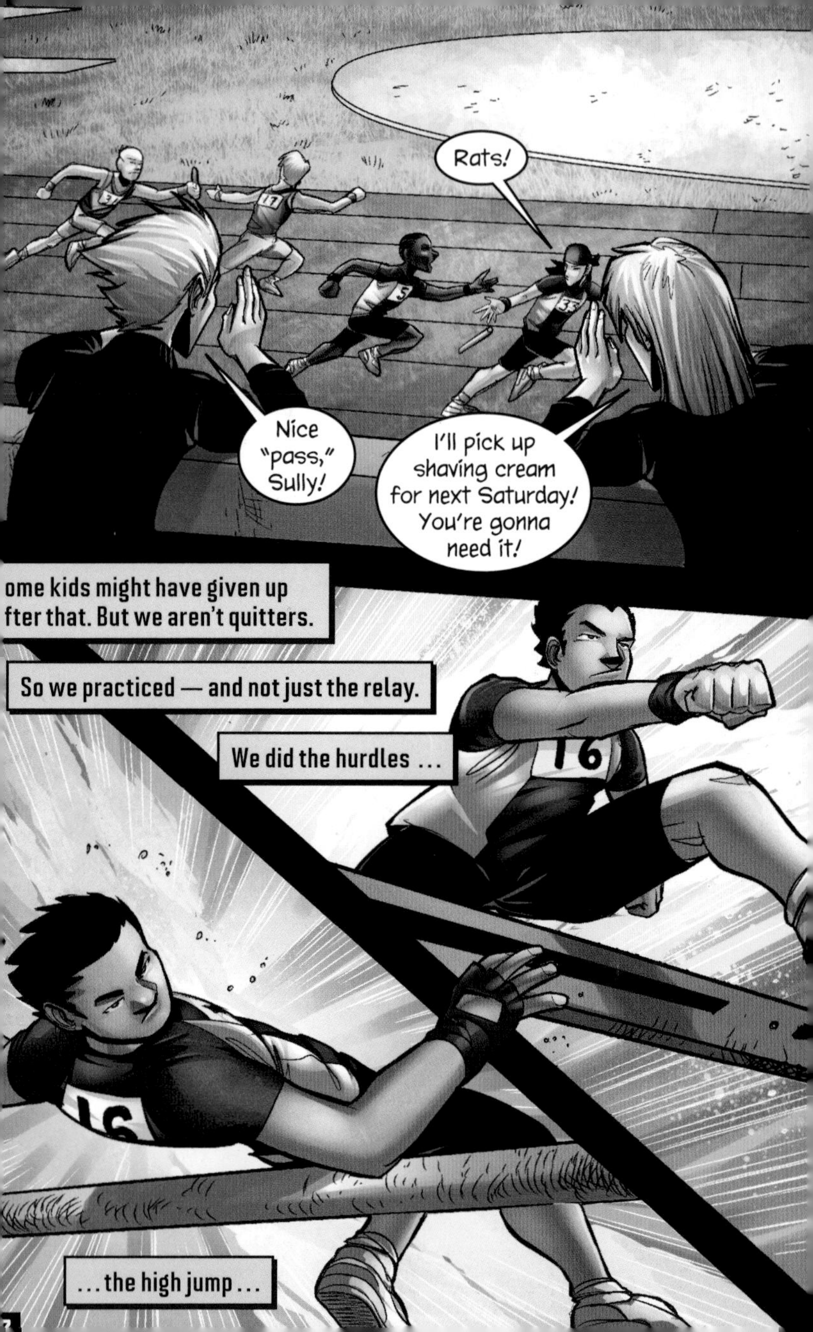
Rats!
Nice "pass," Sully!
I'll pick up shaving cream for next Saturday! You're gonna need it!
ome kids might have given up fter that. But we aren't quitters.
So we practiced — and not just the relay.
We did the hurdles …
… the high jump …

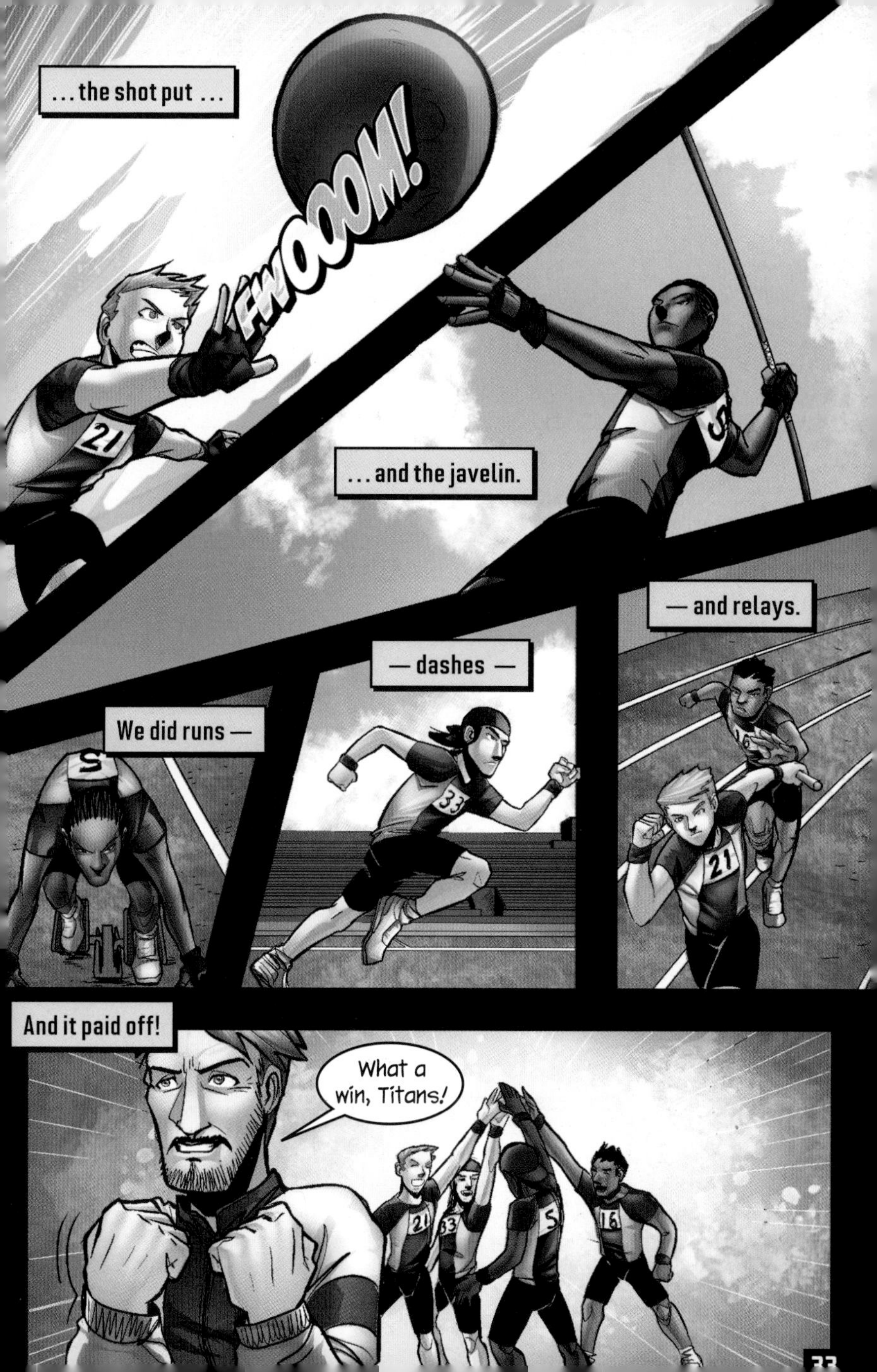
... the shot put ...
FWOOOM!
... and the javelin.
We did runs —
— dashes —
— and relays.
And it paid off!
What a win, Titans!

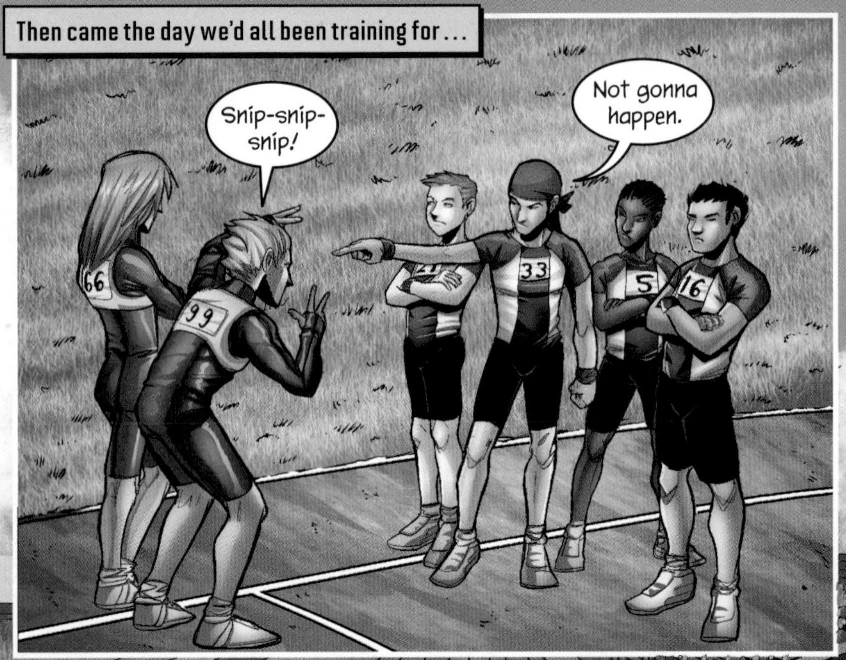
Then came the day we'd all been training for . . .
Snip-snip-snip!
Not gonna happen.
66
99
33
5
16

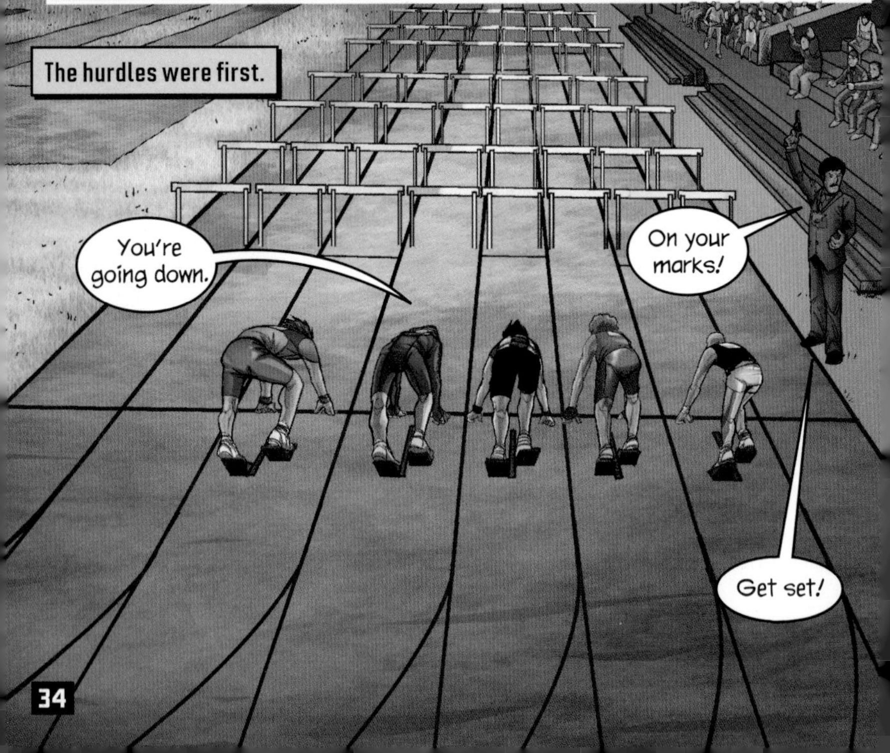
The hurdles were first.
You're going down.
On your marks!
Get set!

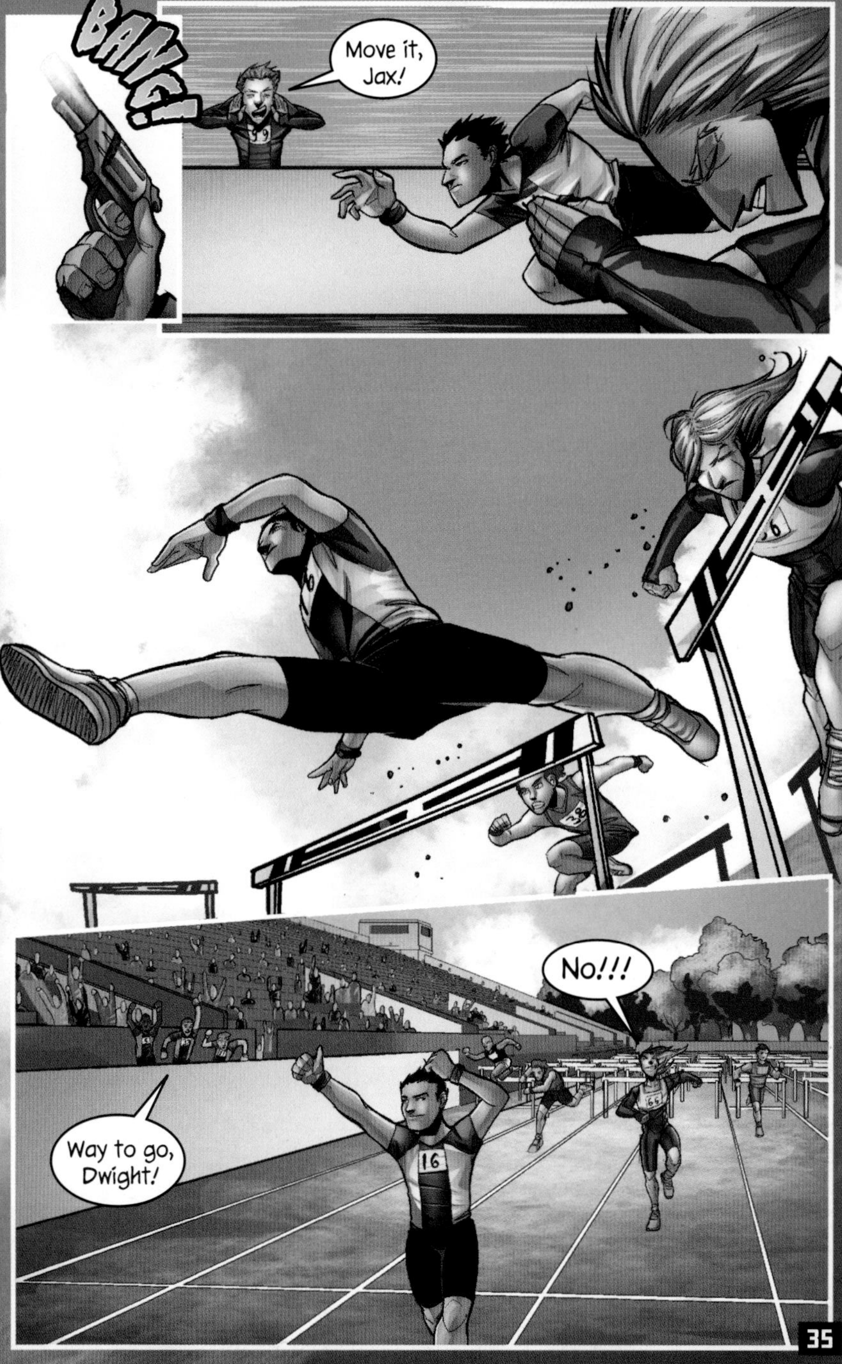
BANG!
Move it, Jax!
No!!!
Way to go, Dwight!

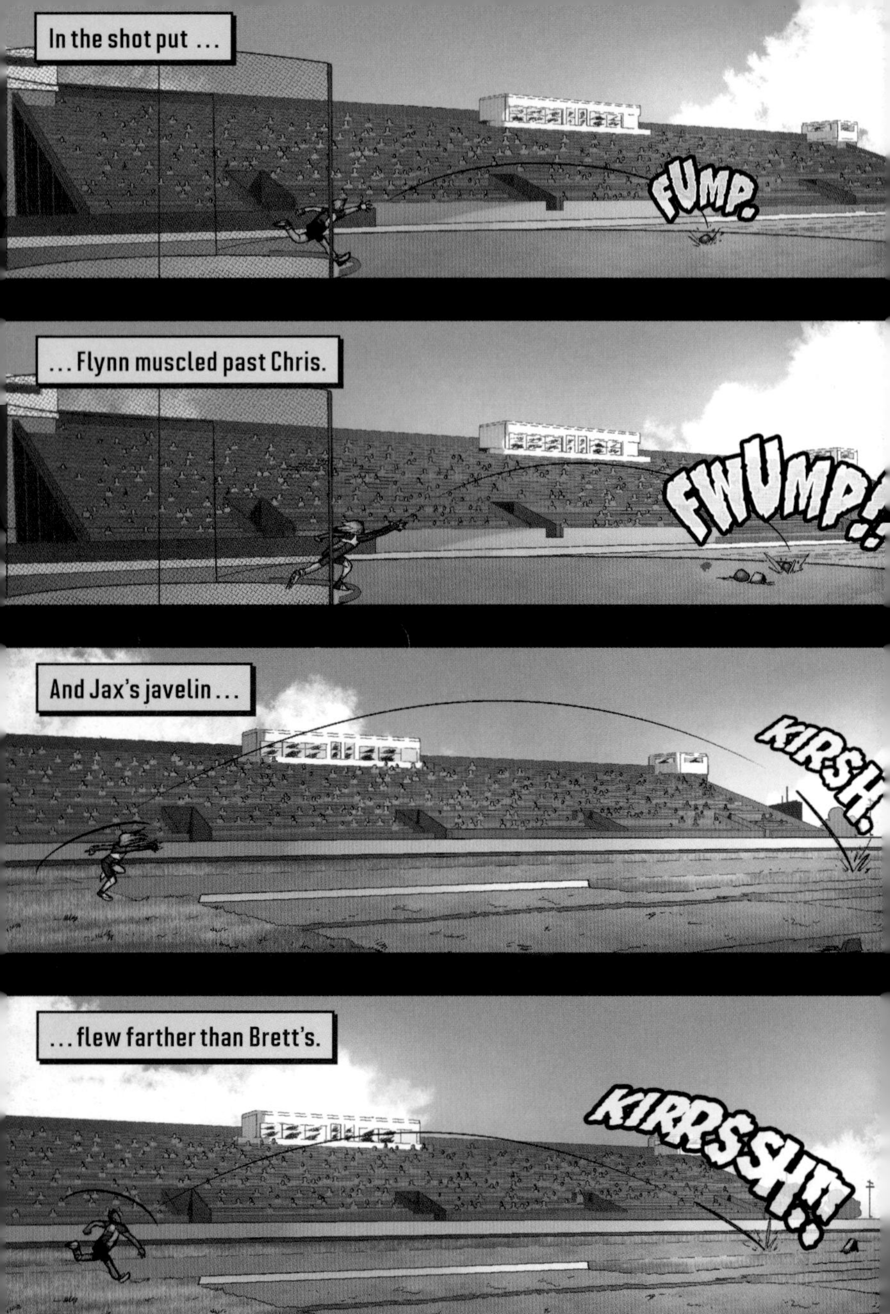
In the shot put ...
FUMP.
... Flynn muscled past Chris.
FWUMP!!
And Jax's javelin...
KIRSH!
... flew farther than Brett's.
KIRRSSH!!

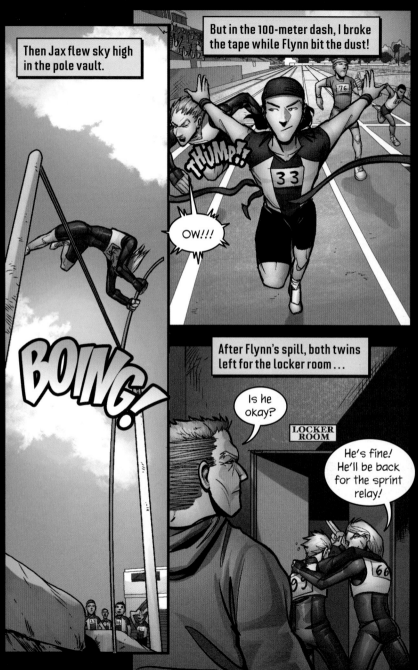

Then Jax flew sky high in the pole vault.

But in the 100-meter dash, I broke the tape while Flynn bit the dust!

THUMP!!

OW!!!

BOING!

After Flynn's spill, both twins left for the locker room...

Is he okay?

LOCKER ROOM

He's fine! He'll be back for the sprint relay!

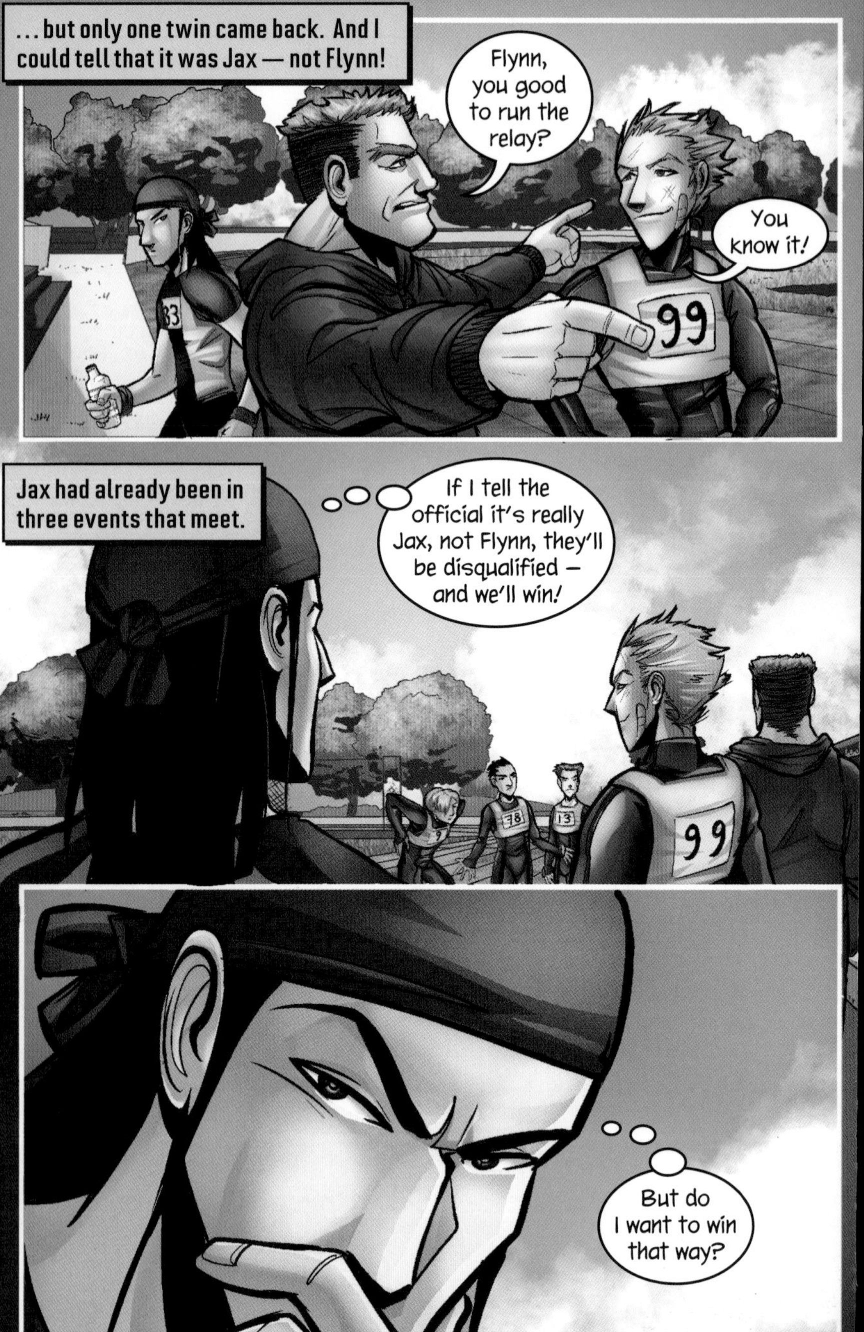
... but only one twin came back. And I could tell that it was Jax — not Flynn!
Flynn, you good to run the relay?
You know it!
99
33
Jax had already been in three events that meet.
If I tell the official it's really Jax, not Flynn, they'll be disqualified — and we'll win!
78
13
99
But do I want to win that way?

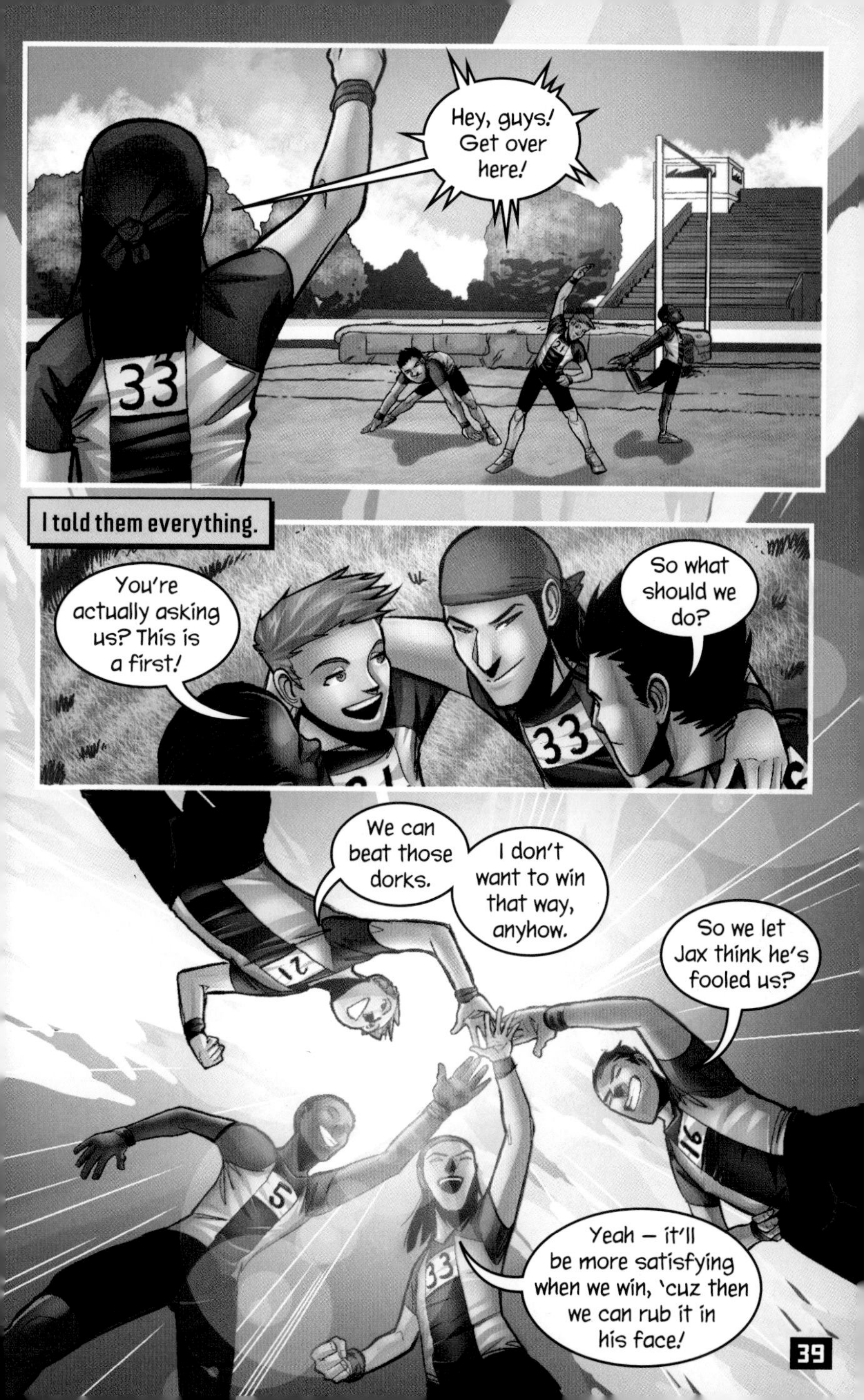
Hey, guys! Get over here!
I told them everything.
You're actually asking us? This is a first!
So what should we do?
We can beat those dorks.
I don't want to win that way, anyhow.
So we let Jax think he's fooled us?
Yeah — it'll be more satisfying when we win, 'cuz then we can rub it in his face!

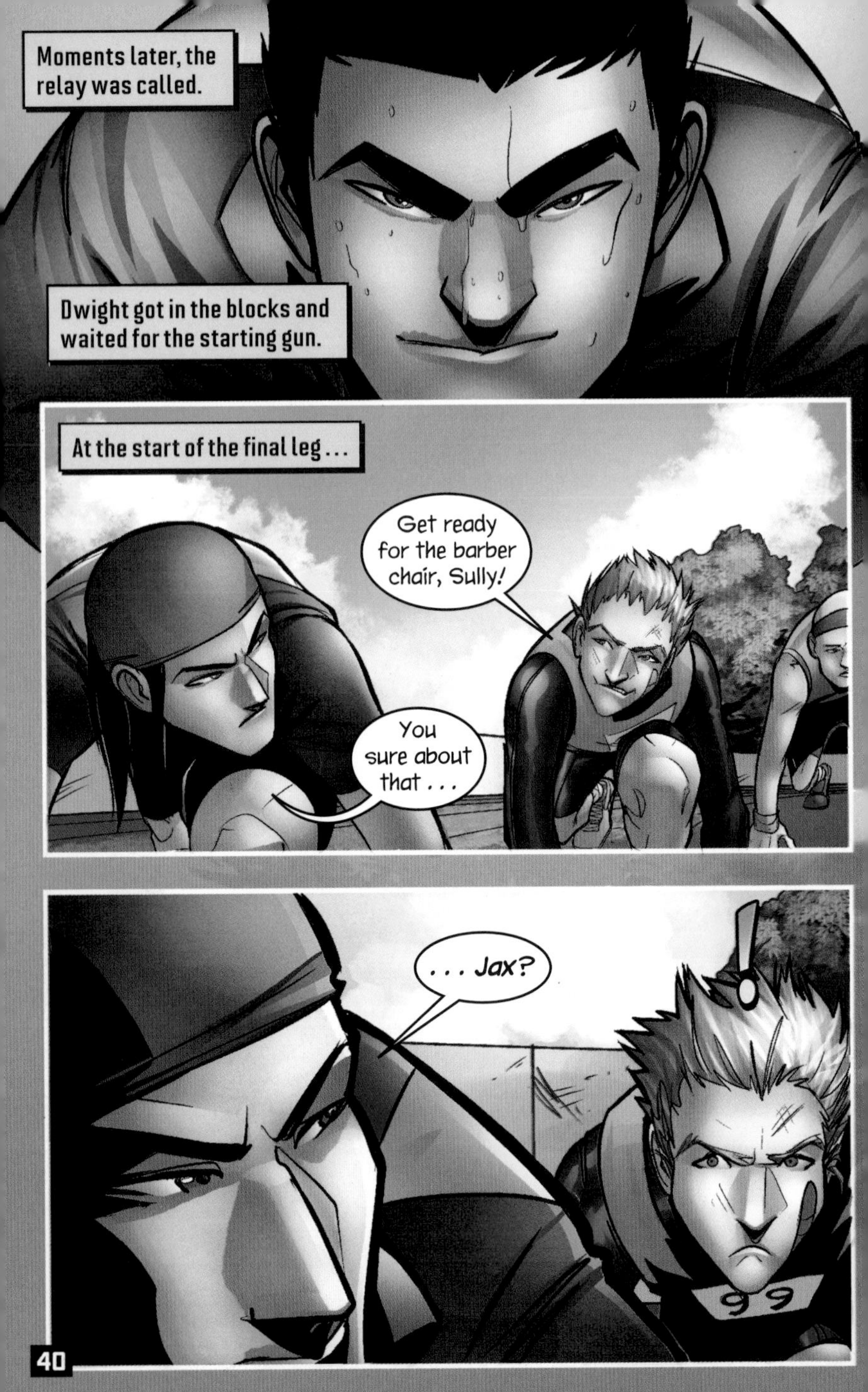
Moments later, the relay was called.
Dwight got in the blocks and waited for the starting gun.
At the start of the final leg . . .
Get ready for the barber chair, Sully!
You sure about that . . .
. . . Jax?

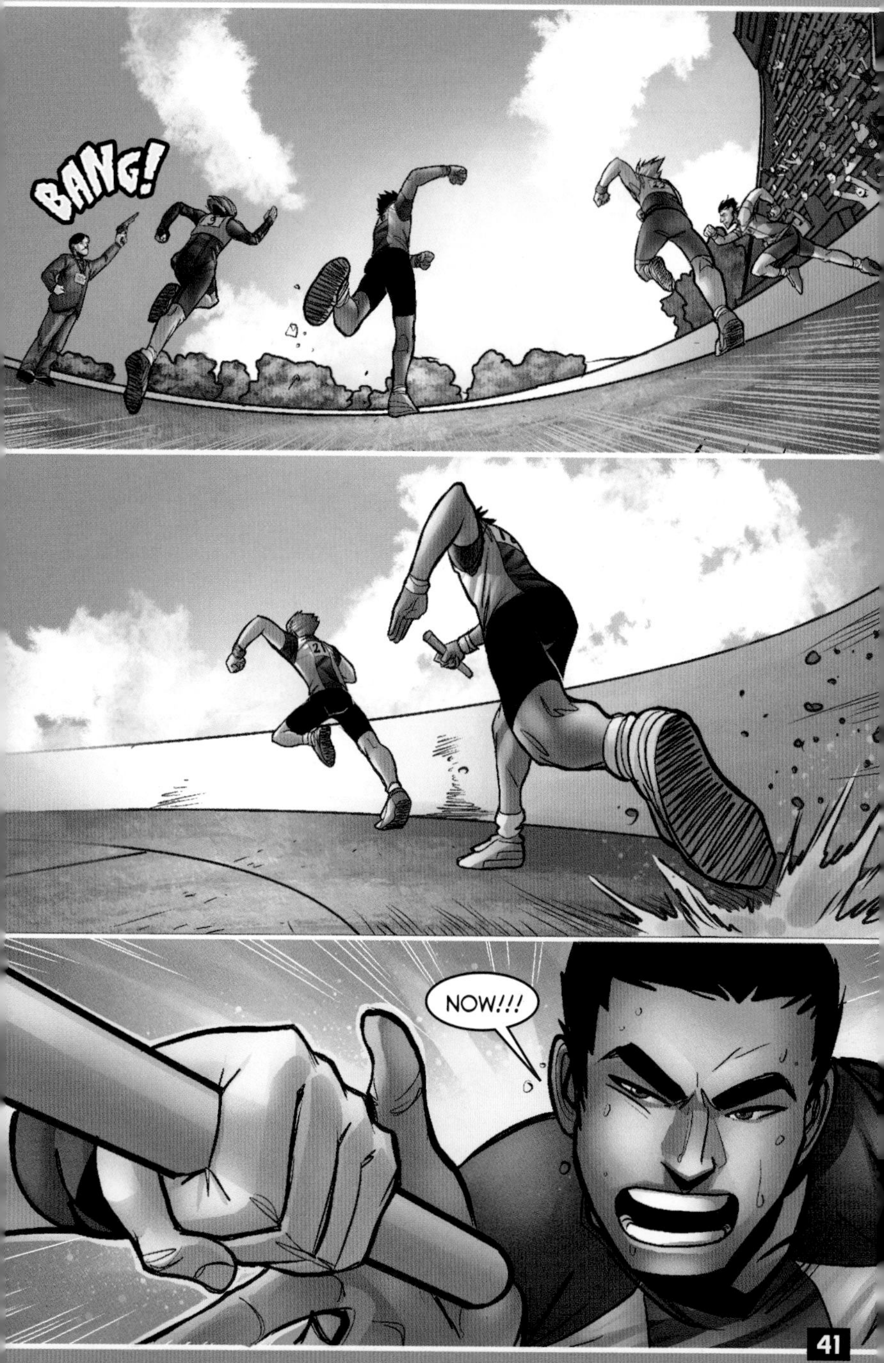
BANG!
NOW!!!

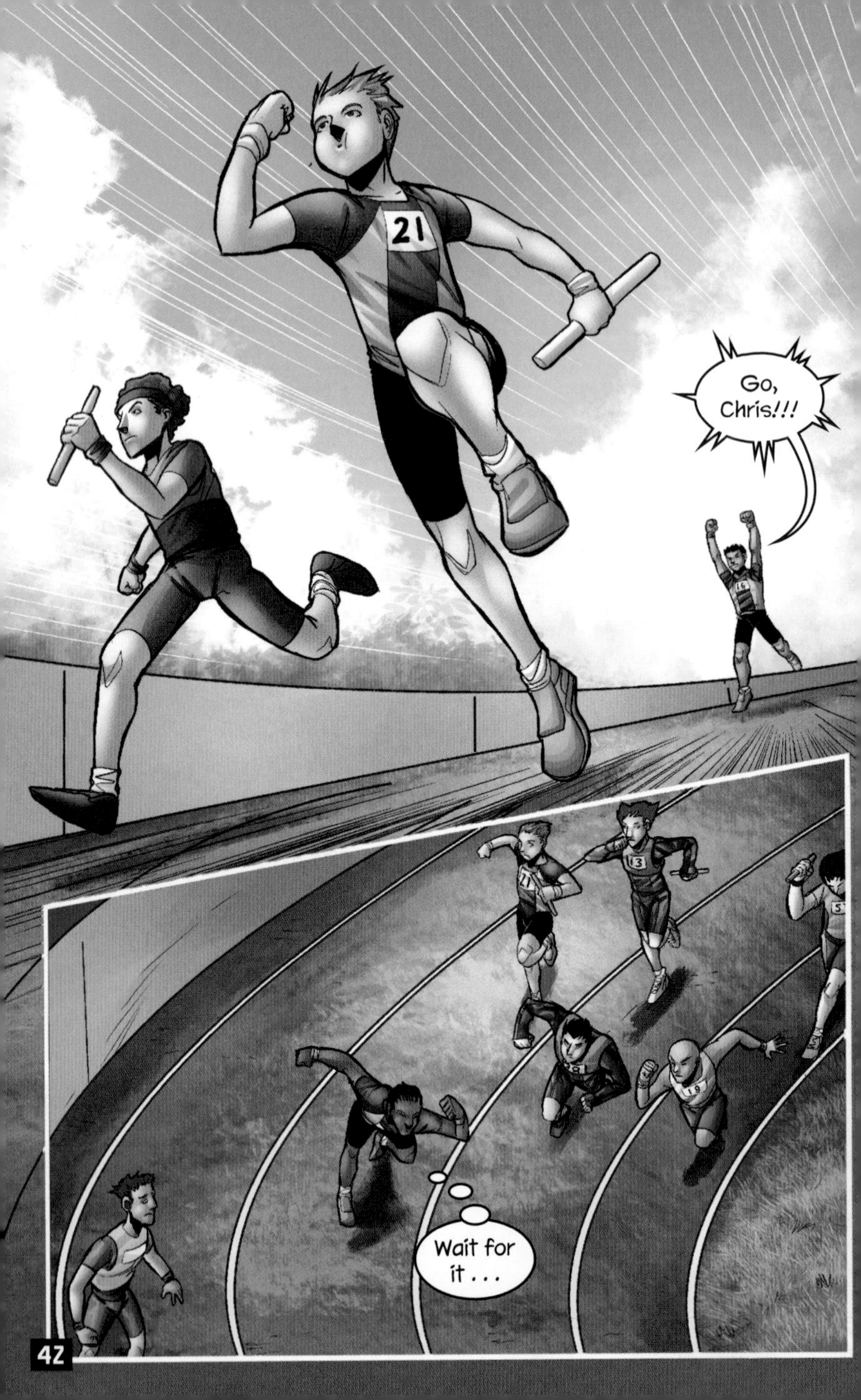
Go, Chris!!!
Wait for it . . .

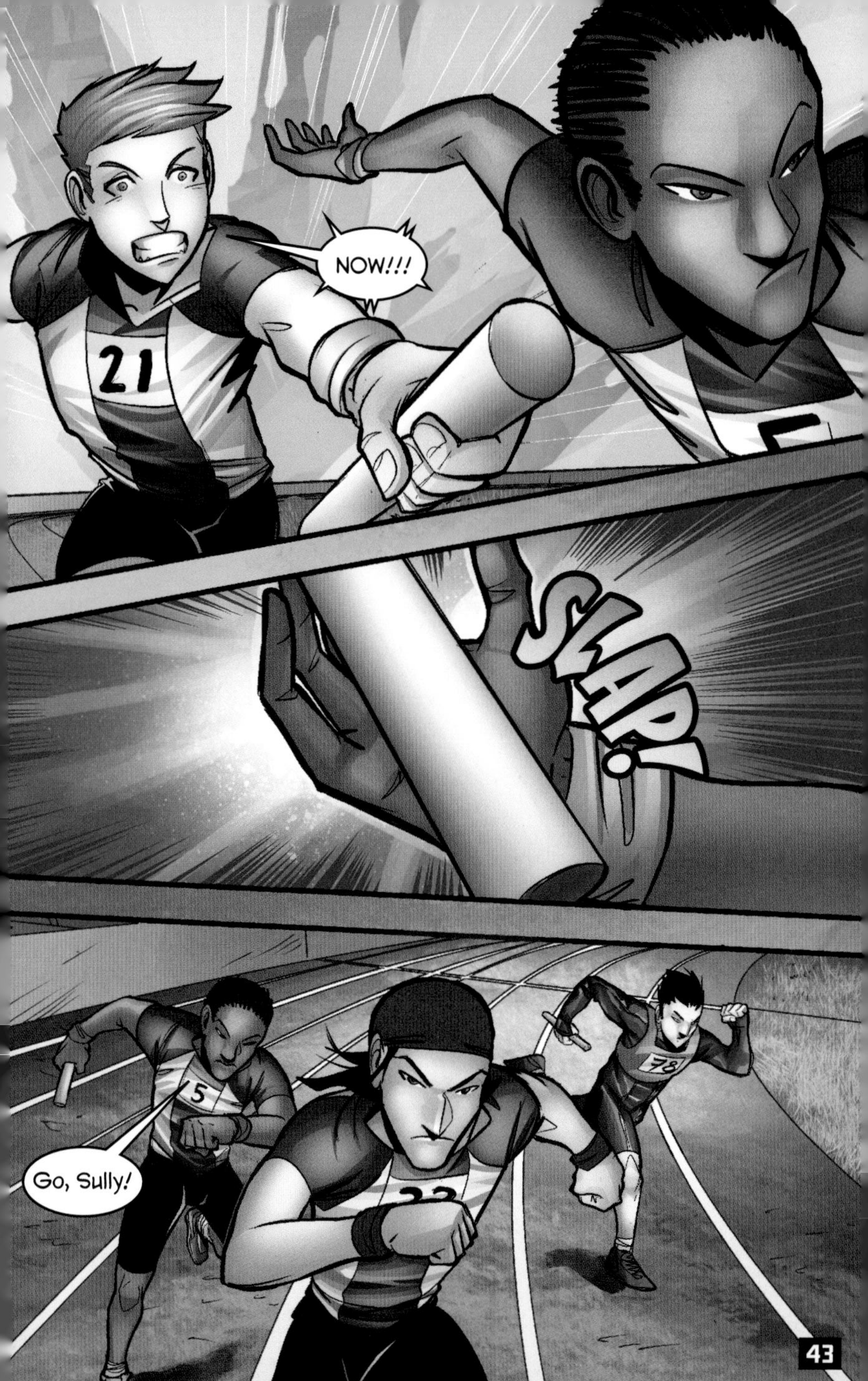
NOW!!!
SLAP!
Go, Sully!

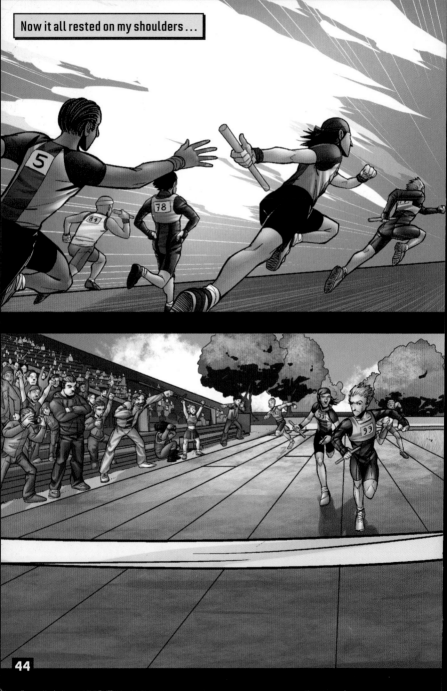

Now it all rested on my shoulders...

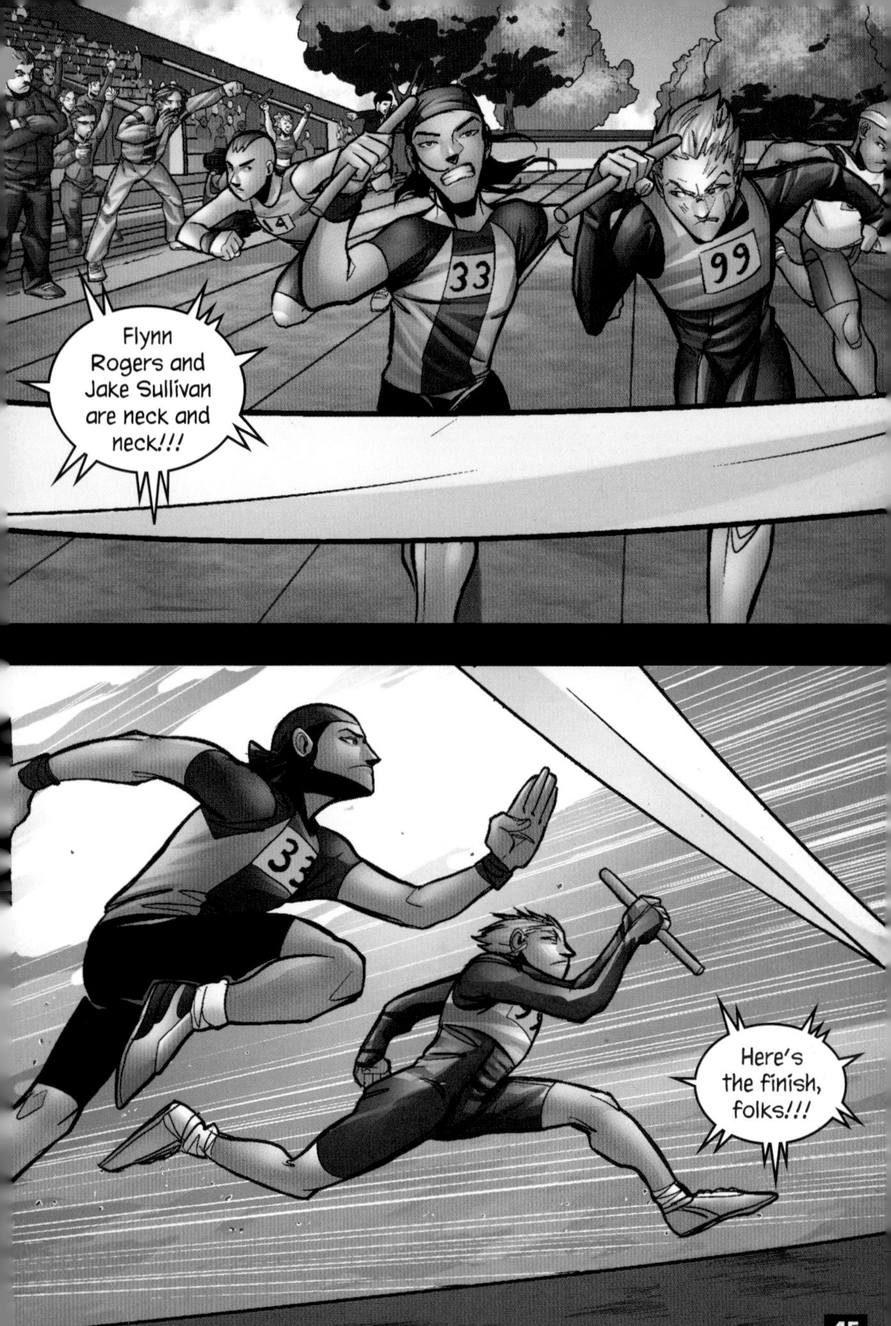
Flynn Rogers and Jake Sullivan are neck and neck!!!
Here's the finish, folks!!!

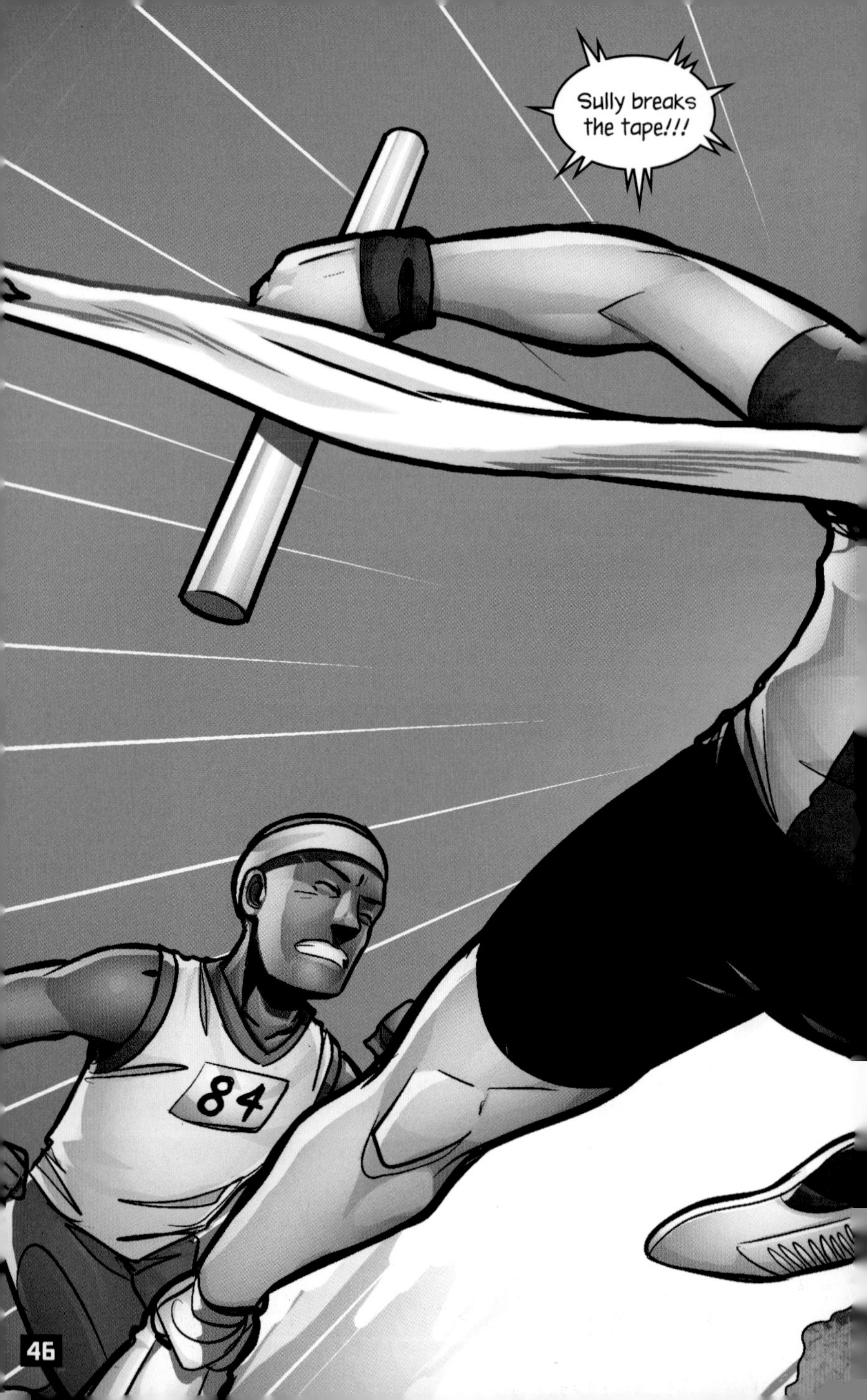
Sully breaks the tape!!!
84

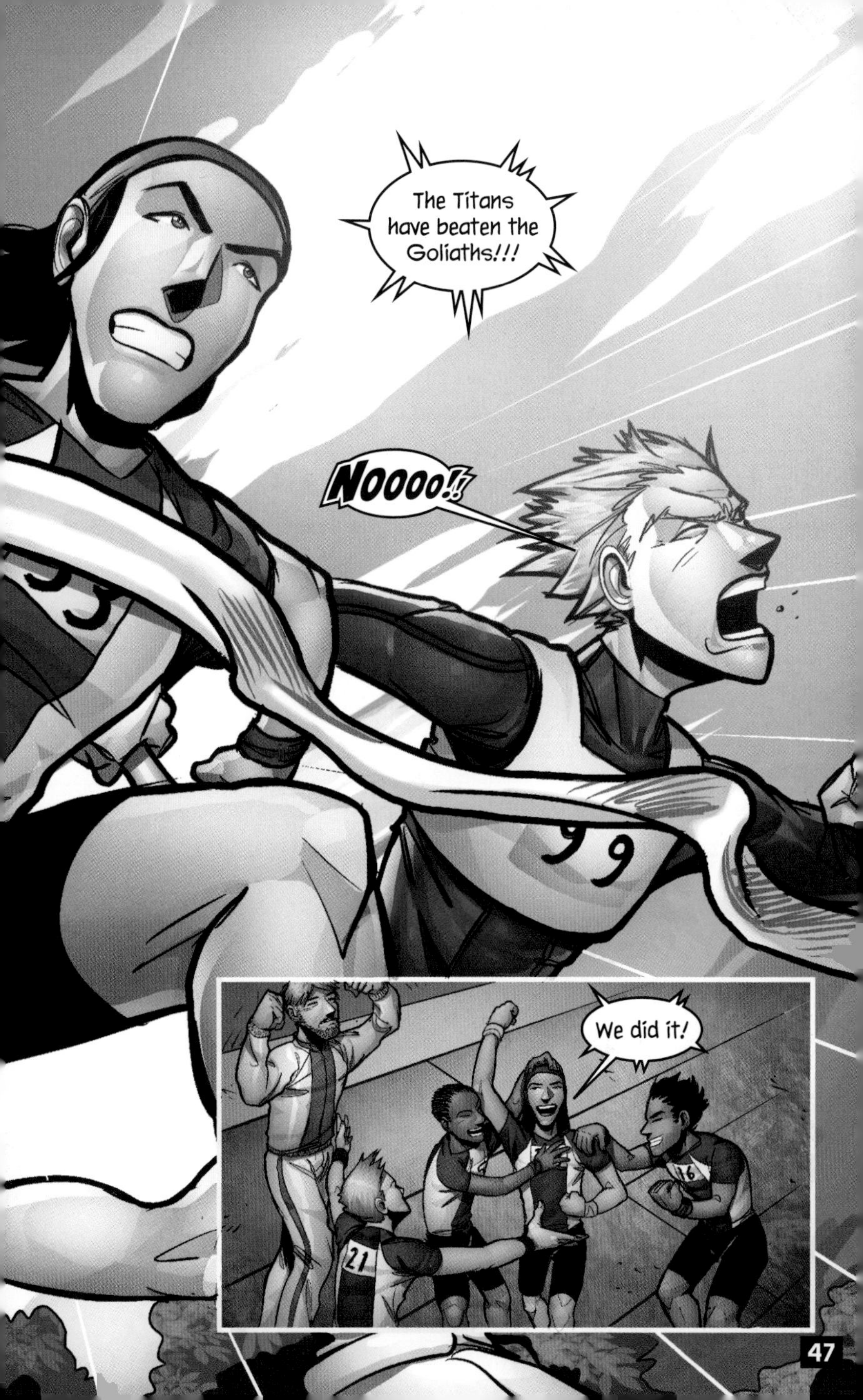
The Titans have beaten the Goliaths!!!
NOOOO!!
We did it!

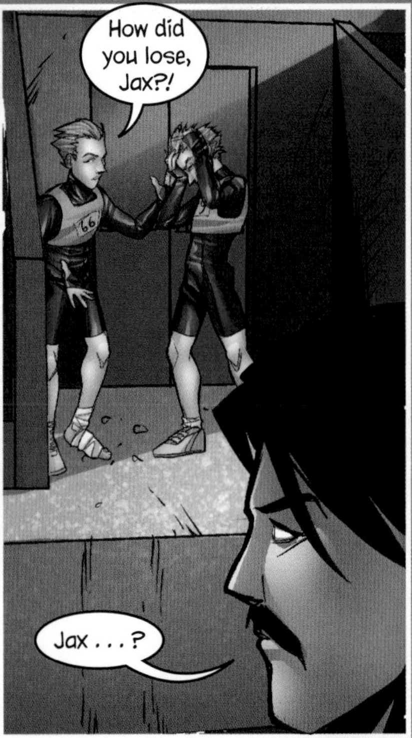
How did you lose, Jax?!
Jax . . . ?

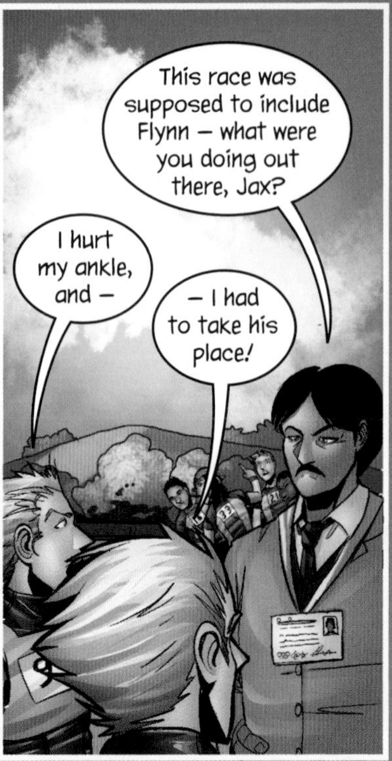
This race was supposed to include Flynn — what were you doing out there, Jax?
I hurt my ankle, and —
— I had to take his place!

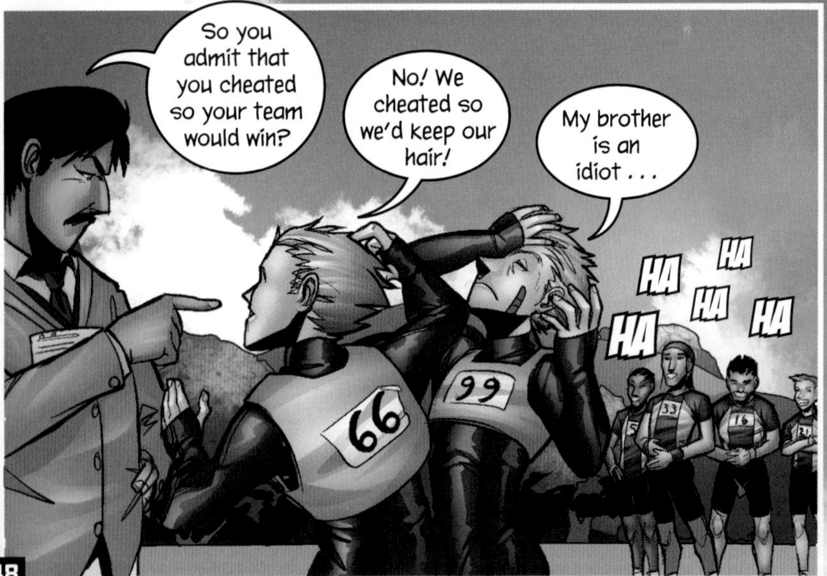
So you admit that you cheated so your team would win?
No! We cheated so we'd keep our hair!
My brother is an idiot . . .
HA HA HA HA HA

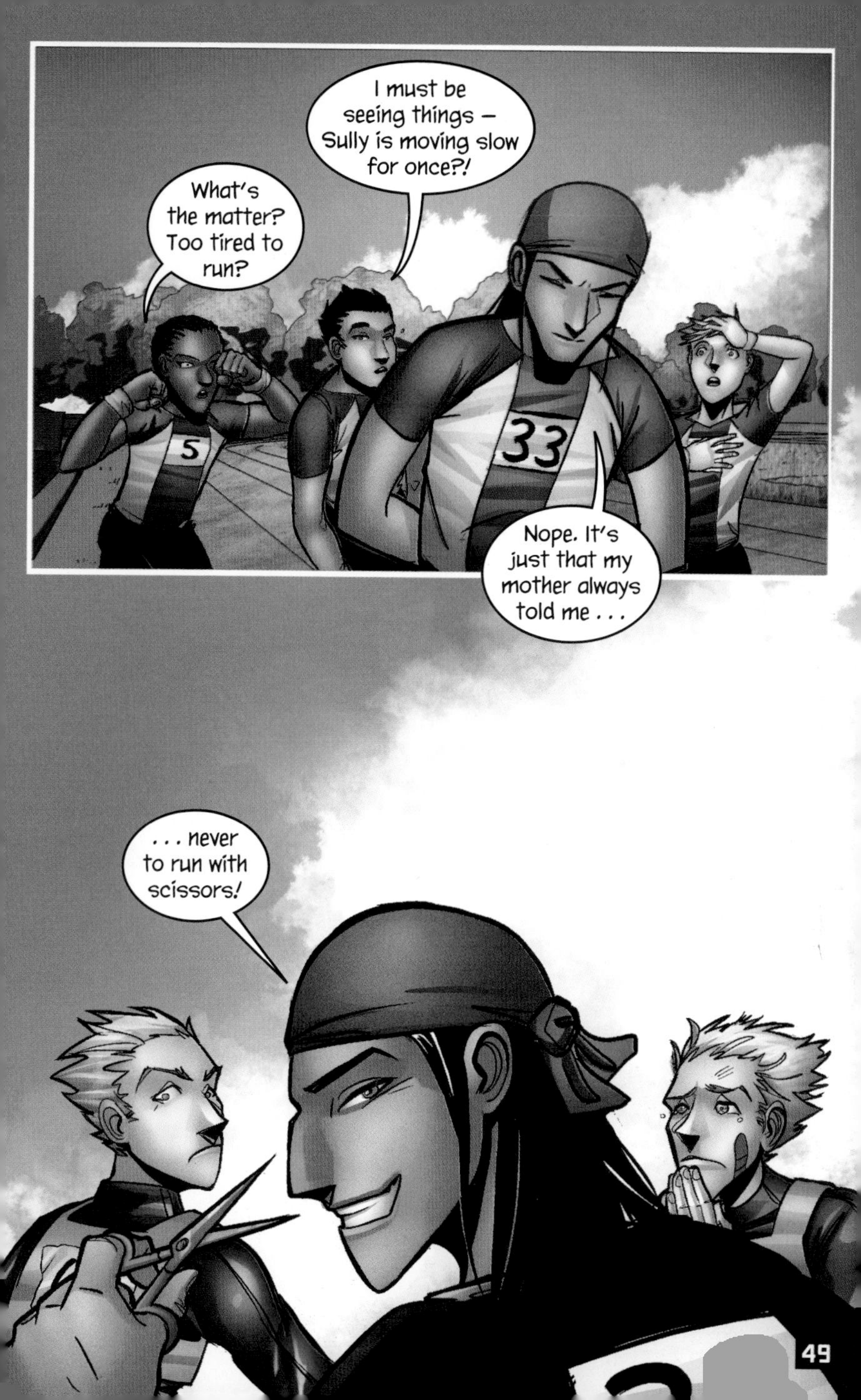
What's the matter? Too tired to run?
I must be seeing things — Sully is moving slow for once?!
Nope. It's just that my mother always told me . . .
. . . never to run with scissors!
5
33

TRACK TEAM TITANS OUTRUN ROGERS TWINS TO SEAL WIN!

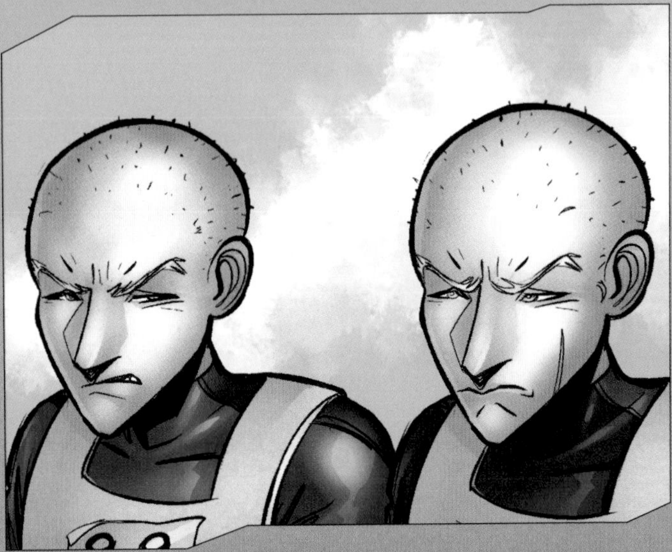

STORY: The Titans got the better of the Goliaths as they rallied from behind to take home first place. Jax and Flynn Rogers both had their share of success, but ultimately their dishonesty cost them a shot at gold. Sully was quoted as saying, "I knew the twins were trying to pull a fast one on us, but we were still quicker!"

Y THE UMBERS

AL RANKINGS:

T PLACE: TITANS
D PLACE: GOLIATHS
D PLACE: BADGERS

Sports Illustrated KIDS

UP NEXT: SI KIDS INFO CENTER

POSTGAME *EXTRA*

WHERE *YOU* ANALYZE THE GAME!

BLZ vs BNS
7-1

TGR vs ROR
13-12

EAG vs BAN
14-7

SPA vs WLD
4-1

BAN vs ROR
21-15

ROR vs LIG
5-1

BLZ vs BNS

Track and Field fans got a real treat today when the Titans faced off against the Goliaths. Let's go into the stands and ask some fans for their opinions on the day's track events...

DISCUSSION QUESTION 1

Which team name do you like better — the Titans or the Goliaths? If you had to pick a name for your school's team, what would you choose? Why?

DISCUSSION QUESTION 2

If you were on the Titans track team, which event would you choose to participate in? What skills do you have that would make you good at it? Talk about it.

WRITING PROMPT 1

Jax and Flynn cheated. Have you ever cheated at something? If not, do you know someone who has cheated? Write about your cheating experience.

WRITING PROMPT 2

Sully manages to convince his friends to try out for the track team. Talk about a time when you convinced someone else to do what you wanted.

INFO CENTER

(kom-puh-TISH-uhn)—rivalry offered by an opponent

(kuhn-DISH-uhn)—something that is needed before another thing can happen

(kuhn-VINSS)—make someone believe you

(KOR-nurd)—got someone into a position that traps them

(diss-KWOL-uh-fye)—prevent someone from taking part in an activity

(PESS-tur)—to keep annoying other people, often asking them something over and over again

(SAT-iss-fye-ing)—if something is satisfying, it makes you feel good or contented

(SWORM)—gather and move in large numbers, or surround and overwhelm in large numbers

(vol-uhn-TEER)—offfer to do something, often for free

CREATORS

Stephanie True Peters › Author

After working more than 10 years as a children's book editor, Stephanie True Peters started writing books herself. She has since written 40 books, including the *New York Times* bestseller *A Princess Primer: A Fairy Godmother's Guide to Being a Princess.* When not at her computer, Peters enjoys playing with her two children, hitting the gym, or working on home improvement projects with her patient and supportive husband, Daniel.

Aburtov › Illustrator

Aburtov has worked in the comic book industry for more than 11 years. In that time, he has illustrated popular characters like Wolverine, Iron Man, Blade, and the Punisher. Recently, Aburtov started his own illustration studio called Graphikslava. He lives in Monterrey, Mexico, with his daughter, Ilka, and his beloved wife. Aburtov enjoys spending his spare time with family and friends.

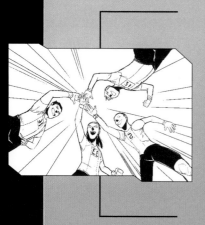

Fares Maese › Inker

Fares Maese is a graphic designer and illustrator. He has worked as a colorist for Marvel Comics, and as a concept artist for the card and role-playing games *Pathfinder* and *Warhammer.* Fares loves spending time playing video games with his Graphikslava comrades, and he's an awesome drum player.

Fernando Cano › Colorist

Fernando Cano is an emerging illustrator born in Mexico City, Mexico. He currently resides in Monterrey, Mexico, where he works as a full-time illustrator and colorist at Graphikslava studio. He has done illustration work for Marvel, DC Comics, and role-playing games like *Pathfinder* from Paizo Publishing. In his spare time, he enjoys hanging out with friends, singing, rowing, and drawing!

Sports Illustrated KIDS GRAPHIC NOVELS

QUICK COMIC

LUKE LAWLESS IN:
BMX BLITZ

Having trouble keeping up with us, Pete?
Actually, Houston . . .
. . . I just know what's up ahead.
Huh?
Yikes!!!
SPLISH!
SPLISH!
SPLISH!

LOVE THIS QUICK COMIC? READ THE WHOLE STORY IN BMX BLITZ – ONLY FROM STONE ARCH BOOKS!

HOT SPORTS.
HOT
FORMAT!

GREAT CHARACTERS BATTLE FOR
SPORTS GLORY IN TODAY'S HOTTEST
FORMAT—GRAPHIC NOVELS!

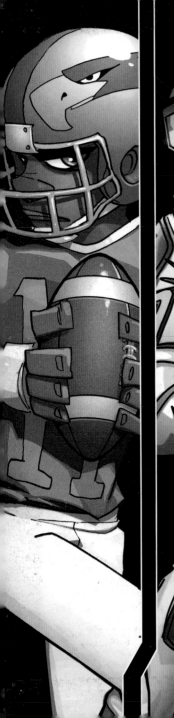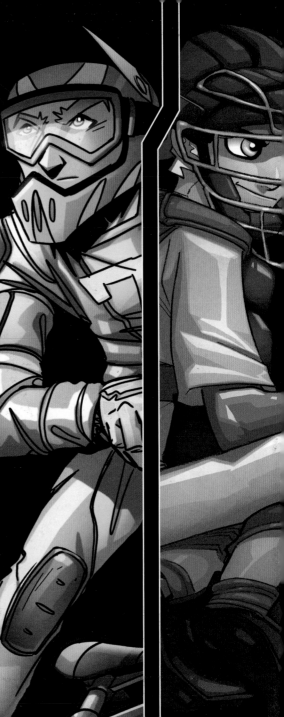